JASON'S

FROM THE BLASCOMB FAMILY CHRONICLES

PASSAGE

By M. R. Compton, Jr.

Edited by Billie Jean Plaster

CABINET CREST
BOOKS

HERON, MONTANA

"UNDER THE BROW OF CLAYTON PEAK"

DEDICATION

HERE'S TO DREAMS AND REALITY, and to that rare place where they meet, where life is sometimes very hard but very much worth living and magic still happens.

SPECIAL THANKS to Chris Bessler, Billie Jean Plaster, Jane Fritz and Randy Wilhelm for their help and advice.

TO MELISSA, EMILY, ANDREW AND JONATHAN; thanks for looks into childhood.

CHRIS, CARMEN, KENT, CINDY, SUSAN, NAN, and the rest of you who have been steadfast friends, fans and supporters, may God be good to you all. I extend my heartfelt gratitude and wish you many blessings.

MOST OF ALL, THIS STORY IS FOR KATIE, for whom it was begun about a million years ago.
                                                                S.C.

265. 9475.   406-897-2356

Published by:
CABINET CREST BOOKS
~~P.O. Box 803~~ 323 N. First
Sandpoint, Idaho 83864

Book design by Chris Bessler and M.R. Compton, Jr.
Cover design by M. R. Compton, Jr.

Manufactured in the United States of America.

PART ONE:

THE LEGEND OF WEST FORK EDDY

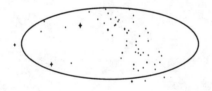

'L ove is patient and kind; love is not jealous or boastful; it is not arrogant or rude. Love does not insist on its own way; it is not irritable or resentful; it does not rejoice at wrong, but rejoices in the right. Love bears all things, believes all things, hopes all things, endures all things."

- St. Paul, in his first letter to the church at Corinth.

All my best,
Sandy Coyote

In the last, red light of the sun, Jason thought he saw a tear giltter on Sara's cheek

THE
ACQUISITION

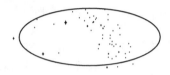

BEFORE THE WAGON ROLLED TO A STOP, Sarah knew which way Caleb would go after he looped the reins on the brake handle. Across the dusty street from Corbin's Store was a tamarack-rail corral used for sorting stock into the railroad loading pens and, on the Fourth of July, for the exciting foolishness of grown men tangling with green horses. In the corral, Dick Hancock was cursing a sweat-covered young stallion. Hancock's chunky face was red with anger and exertion. The sharp smells of summer dust, green manure and a heated horse filled the air.

The horse on Hancock's rope was wild, dragging the big man around the pen, fighting the loop around its neck. The stallion was off the ground as much as on it. His neck rippled, straining against the rope. Ponderously graceful, made heavy by fatigue, he lunged and fought his captor.

He was the kind of animal Caleb always stopped to watch and dream of owning. He seemed to have flowed out of the ground. Sarah, watching from the wagon seat, imagined bones of chiseled stone, flesh of firm red earth and hide fused from the golden sand in the pools in West Fork Creek.

The horse's harsh breathing, the thud of his hooves and Hancock's grunts of effort were the only sounds in a hot July afternoon. The young men and boys on the fence were silent, tense. They had gathered to watch Hancock make good on a boast that he would break the stallion, and not a one of them liked the way things were going. Caleb's two young shadows, Bill and Jon, slipped from the back of the wagon and joined him at the fence to watch through the rails.

Sarah saw Caleb's shoulders hunch in sympathy with the horse's pain, and she started down from the wagon seat, sensing his mounting rage. "Caleb," she found herself saying aloud, "it's not your horse." Sarah was halfway to the fence when she saw the leash chain hanging from Hancock's wrist, and she began to run when he raised it overhead. Before Sarah could reach her husband, Hancock slashed the animal across the face and Caleb was gone, vaulting over the fence and sprinting toward the man and horse.

"William, take care of Jonathan," Sarah barked to the wide-eyed boys as she clambered over the rails, "and stay out of the corral!"

The men perched on the fence began to yell at the prospect of a fight, but Hancock did not hear. He was whirling the chain for another swing at the horse when Caleb hit him in the ribs. The blow loosened Hancock's grip on the lariat and raised a cheer from the crowd. The rope tore at Hancock's gloved hand, and friction made the leather sizzle. Hancock staggered and went down as the stallion bolted away to the far side of the pen.

The men tumbled over and over in the dust, coming to a stop against the fence with Caleb astride Hancock, one hand on his throat and the other raised to strike. Caleb was cold mad and breathing hard.

"Hancock," he said, "I ought to take that chain to you."

"Get offa me, Blascomb," Hancock growled, bucking with his legs "before I tear ya' limb from limb."

Sarah stood panting beside the struggling pair, not quite sure what to do, but she knew she didn't want Caleb arrested.

She made her voice firm. "Caleb!"

Hancock tried to twist from under him. Caleb squeezed with his legs around the bigger man's ribs and drew a wheeze of pain from him.

"Caleb, that's enough!" Sarah said. "You'll break something."

"That wouldn't hurt my feelings a bit," Caleb said through clenched teeth, looking down at Hancock. "I'd like to tie his back legs up around his ears."

"Good God, man, don't do that." Hancock, frightened now, was beginning to think that Caleb could do just what he threatened.

"Caleb..." Sarah's reasonable tone was fast becoming unreasonable. Caleb relented and clambered to his feet, leaving Hancock in the deep dust panting and puffing.

Hancock rolled onto his side, holding his belly as if he were sick. "My good God, man. What the hell do ya think you're doing?"

Caleb didn't answer. He didn't even hear Hancock. He was walking away, making slow clucking sounds to the horse that stood quivering against the far rail.

Sarah watched Caleb move across the pen. With a trace of humor in her voice, she said quietly to the man on the ground, "Mr. Hancock, your good God is all that saved you from the thrashing you deserve."

Through the rail, Caleb's two sons watched their father.

"Is Pop going to try to ride 'im?" Jon asked, wondering how even his father could approach such a wild thing as the horse that stood snorting and blowing before them.

Bill knew not to spook the big animal. "I don't think so," he whispered, "at least, not this minute."

They looked at each other and grinned, enjoying their private joke. They knew their father and the special place horses held in his heart, and they knew from his expression as he sidled up to the big horse that he was smitten.

At Caleb's approach, the horse tensed up and danced along the fence, wary and defiant. The lariat hung loose, and

Caleb could see the work it had done. Rope burns encircled the horse's neck. The new slash across his forehead was matched by an identical, perpendicular line, just healed. There was another long, hairless mark down the left haunch, pink, freshly grown over.

"Hey, horse," Caleb said, quietly. The horse bounced away toward one corner of the corral and Caleb let him go into it. The horse went by the boys and they could smell him, and feel the heat coming off his body.

"Hey, horsey horse," Caleb said, in a low, warm voice. The horse looked at him from one eye, standing sideways, cocked to go.

"Hey, horse," Caleb murmured. He walked slowly toward the stallion, humming and holding out both hands.

"Hey, horse. Now you stand still, old horsey horse. Just stand there a minute while I look you over. Don't be running over me."

Caleb kept talking softly as he approached, holding out his hands to the horse, reassuring him by steady, slow talk and movement.

"Hey horse," Caleb said, nearly under his breath, as he let the stallion smell his right hand. His left touched the horse's flank, and the stallion flinched away, turning on the fence and skittering off a couple of steps. Caleb clicked his tongue against his teeth. The horse stopped and watched.

His sides were heaving and sweat-caked. His face was bleeding. He was quivering from adrenaline fear had pumped into his system, but he was curious, attracted by this calm, quiet man. Caleb, though still angry at the animal's mistreatment, chuckled. It was a laugh of joy, the kind of joy an art lover might feel standing in front of an original painting by Renoir. This was a horse among horses, a stellar animal of such worth he was nearly priceless, but worthless in the wrong hands. Hancock would never subdue this animal by force. The horse would die first, or have to be neutered.

"Hey, horsey horse," Caleb murmured, "stand still, old horse, be still."

Bill and Jon watched silently as the stallion let Caleb approach. Caleb again let the horse sniff his right hand and his left went under the lariat and pulled the rope gently off.

Hancock had pulled himself off the ground and stood against the fence, seething. "Who in the hell do you think you are, Blascomb?" he yelled. "He's my horse. Get away from him, or I'll get the law on you!"

At Hancock's shout, the horse bolted down the fence past the boys, tilting along the rail at full speed. He cut the corner and suddenly he was bearing down on Hancock.

Sprinting to cut him off, Caleb tried to distract the charging animal. "Hey, horse!"

Hancock turned and ran, in his panic ignoring the safety of the fence.

As the stallion thundered toward Hancock, Sarah, wide-eyed, scooted up the fence and over, then raced down the outside of the fence. The horse, Caleb and Sarah all arrived where Hancock stood at the same time. In the jumble of the moment, Caleb, shouting and waving his arms, stepped between Hancock and the horse and Sarah reached through the fence and grabbed Caleb's shirt. She pulled him against the fence, her fright turned to power and she held him out of harm's way with all her strength.

Hancock dove to the ground and tried in vain to get under the bottom rail of the fence. Finding that futile, he covered his head with his arms and pulled his legs under him.

Confused by the jumble of arms and legs, and perhaps sensing impending freedom, the stallion hesitated slightly, then gathered and launched itself toward the top of the fence. He hit the top rail and sent it flying. Then he was over and gone.

Sarah let go of Caleb's shirt as the horse escaped. Climbing quickly to the top of the fence, Caleb watched the horse race away across the meadow and clear the field's barbed-wire fence.

The fence-sitters, who had watched in silence since Caleb began to approach the horse, exploded in cheers as the horse disappeared into the forest. Then they began to gather at the corner to listen to what Caleb Blascomb might have to say to Dick Hancock.

Hancock's fear turned to anger. He was livid. "Just who the hell do you think you are, coming in here and fooling with my animal. If it hadn't been for you, I'd have him snubbed up by now. I've been working toward it for two weeks. Today was the day and you ruined it."

"Dick," Caleb said, quietly, "you're right. Today was the day."

He paused and leaned into the fence, looking through the rails to where the horse had vanished into the trees. He tracked the most likely route the horse would take, trying to guess about where it would stop running. Finally, he turned back to Hancock.

"Dick, today that horse was going to kill you, and you were lucky enough to have us here to save you."

"What the hell you talking about, Blascomb?" Hancock sputtered. "Listen, you little..."

"Mr. Hancock," Sarah interrupted coldly, "please be good enough not to swear in front of the children."

The two boys had run to join their mother during the melee in the corner. Hancock glared through the fence at Sarah and the two boys, who stared back. The image struck Caleb as funny; three pairs of eyes, each its own hue and at its own level, staring through the narrowly spaced rails. The center pair of eyes blinked, slowly, and that nearly made Caleb laugh.

"Yes, Dick, it was lucky we were here and saved your life. Otherwise, they would have to destroy that horse, and sell your farm at Sheriff's sale to pay for your funeral and the wake. Your widow would go off to Spokane to start again. Probably would marry a clerk, or some such...,"

Sarah winced and bit her lip to keep from laughing.

"...and all the work you've done on your place would fall into dust, like those logging camps up on the flats. My goodness, think of the calamity we've helped you avoid."

10

Hancock stared incredulously at Caleb, and up on the fence, someone guffawed. Caleb glanced sharply at the gawkers, favoring them with a stern look. Most of them had worked for Caleb at one time or another.

"I'd think," Caleb said slowly, "that you would have something to do at home."

"Not me," one of them piped up, a skinny blond boy of about 18.

Caleb's look at the boy was steady and a little on the chilly side. "If you'd like, I'll send a note along with some suggestions, Sunny."

Sunny blushed and grinned, and said, "Oops. I guess I do hear my mother calling, after all." Caleb was known to be fair … and firm.

The rest of the hangers-on laughed and began to dissipate, leaving Caleb and his family and Hancock at the corral.

"How much do you want for that horse?" Caleb asked.

Caleb kept his eyes on Hancock, but he guessed that if he were to look at Sarah at that moment he might wither and die on the spot. He knew Sarah was about sick and tired of the horse business. He also knew the stallion was the finest animal he had seen in an age, and knew that he had a huge advantage he must press forward with now. He hadn't time to reason with his wife just then.

Caleb needn't have worried. Sarah was gazing after the departing crowd, a puzzled look on her face.

The last to go was a slim, swarthy young man of perhaps 19. He was a stranger to Sarah, but something about him struck a familiar note and he walked uncertainly as he left, staring back at Caleb as if he knew him.

Something about him disturbed Sarah, and she wondered what it was. She finally decided it was his eyes. By all his other features, they should have been brown, but they were piercing blue. They made him look somehow haunted. Sarah glanced back to the men in the corral, and when she looked again, the boy was gone.

By that time, Caleb owned another horse.

11

HORSE TRADERS wondered sometimes how they could be convinced the horses they touted as thoroughbreds were really plug ponies and lame pack animals to be saved from the glue factory by Caleb Blascomb of the West Fork Horse Retirement Home. After Caleb led the poor broken-down thing away, they realized they had sold a prime horse for a dog food price and felt guilty for charging so much.

Such was the plight of Dick Hancock. When he looked at the incident later, out of the light of the flaming wreck of his pride, it was a relief to be rid of the horse, for he realized Caleb was right. It was either him or the horse. And now, the horse was gone, God knew how far up into the Cabinet Mountains. A cougar would have him by the end of the day — and good riddance, Hancock thought.

When Caleb wrote the draft for $75 on Sand River State Bank, Hancock was as nearly grateful as a man like him can be, though he had paid much more for the horse two months before at a sale in Bozeman. He'd salvaged a little out of the deal.

FOR SUCH A HOT DAY, the ride home from Sand River was on the chilly side. Three-year-old Alicia had napped in the wagon through all the excitement, and was unhappy at being awakened by her bothers. Sarah had other thoughts about how to use $75, and was not happy about the purchase of another horse, especially one not even in hand.

The silence stretched a long mile up the dusty road toward the West Fork before Alicia, an intuitive little girl, asked "Daddy, did you buy another horse?" She said it with such inflection, and with such intent and seriousness that the rest of them could not help but laugh, and the chill was partly broken.

Caleb quietly sighed and said, "Yes, little girl, I did, and what a horse he is." His eyes swung up the ascending bulk of the Cabinets, trying to discern where the horse might be at that moment.

He smiled across his daughter at Sarah. "I'm sorry, Sarah.

I know it's quite a risk, but I also know that horse. When I bring him home, he'll make the West Fork."

Sarah had quietly decided that the curtains in the living room were really still quite fashionable and her old cotton frock could be worked up into a new dress for Alicia, but she was still angry.

"Yes, Caleb, when you bring him home."

He grimaced at the barbs in Sarah's voice and clucked up the team, gently slapping the long reins on the big Morgan rumps, and wrapped his free arm around Alicia. After a while, Sarah relented, laying her hand on his arm. Bill began "Bright Coral Bells" after that, and they sang the round up the grade toward the West Fork as the summer sun sank behind them, turning the Cabinets to green gold.

The cool zephyr felt good after the hot day. Caleb, driving and singing, hesitated when a flash of golden-brown turned on the mountainside. He pulled the down-mountain breeze deep within him.

He thought he smelled horse on the wind.

LABAN'S LABOR

CALEB WAS GONE BEFORE LIGHT, riding down the road toward Sand River on Laban, a big tough gray who had been with him since the Beaverhead days. He wasn't much for looks or speed, but when time came for such things, it was Laban's pride and privilege to carry the children of the West Fork on their first solo ride.

He was a calm old gelding with great strength and mountain skills. His big feet were sure and rock steady on narrow paths and steep hillsides and he was unshakably calm. He would stand for a cat or a bear without panic, and took saddle or pack frame without protest. For those qualities, Caleb chose Laban for the day's special job.

Caleb closed the gate behind him and Laban trotted up the road and darkness began to thin at the edges of the world where the rocky serration of high ridges around the West Fork and Sand River rasp against the sky. The stars faded against the growing grayness until only the brightest and the remnants of the last full moon were left. Laban's hooves lifted puffs of dust that fell back to the ground in the cool morning air, leaving a low haze and big "U's" in the road and soft echoes off the trees.

The light in the sky fell softly to earth, piling slowly around dark trunks and settling on black branches until individual trees appeared in the forest, and then the peaks to the north were lit with the orange fire that marks the full ascent of day. When that bright illumination reached a place half-way down the Cabinets to the valley floor, one could see well enough to track a horse through heavy timber, and this was when Caleb came to the place where the young runaway had crossed the road the day before.

Studying the trail the horse had left, Caleb saw he was unshod, but that was not surprising. The thought of holding one of those wild hooves in hand would not set well with any farrier. The horse had stumbled crossing the barrow pit, but it hadn't hurt him. The trail led into the forest. Caleb remounted Laban and followed it in.

Later, after the sun had spread to the valley floor, Caleb looked back from a hillside above the town. Standing in blooming beargrass, Laban's nose turned white from pollen as he sampled the flowers. Spread below, Caleb saw Sand River and the Clark Fork beyond the town, with the railroad running between. Black smoke from an engine marked passage of the morning freight from where it egressed the Clark Fork canyon and through the trees along the river to where it revealed itself and flashed by the Sand River station. Seconds later, a rumble and the shriek of a steam whistle drifted up the mountain and reached them.

Caleb sat astride Laban about where he had seen the glint of color on the hillside the evening before. Here were grassy open patches, stands of virgin larch and fir and areas of young second-growth trees and brush, 10 to 15 years old. Gray-white spars of fire killed timber towered up out of the regrowth, reminders of August, 1910, when the great fires swept the Cabinets and the Coeur d'Alenes, three years before Caleb and Sarah arrived.

He could see the West Fork, both the stream and the ranch he named after the creek. Of his 160 acres, part was burned in 1910 and part was spared. They worked at clearing the burned areas for hay ground and grazing, used fire-killed timber for buildings, fencing and firewood and grubbed out the stumps one by one with dynamite and team and tenacity. The little clearing he could see seemed hardly indicative of all the work that had gone into it when set against the whole green valley, but he took comfort in that little speck. It was his doing, and it was home for him and his family.

He took out his binoculars and scanned his fields. He had to smile when Bill and Jon came into sight. Though he couldn't see every detail, he knew it was them, and he knew they were carrying fishing poles and a lunch in a knapsack. He watched them into the woods at the edge of the orchard. They were headed to the mouth of the West Fork, where the creek ran into the Clark Fork. Inside of an hour, Caleb would wager, one of them would pull a big, brown, spotted char out of the whirlpool that turned forever clockwise downstream of the big rock that sat where the creek entered the river. The bait today would be immature grasshoppers, small and green, just big enough to cover the hook, presented with enough skill to fool one of the big trout.

Sarah and the children would have fresh fish for dinner, and he would have the same, but not char. His dinner would be cutthroat from the upper West Fork.

CALEB KNEW there was not much for a horse to eat on that hillside. He had been everywhere on the West Fork. Like an ant tracing the branches of an oak, Caleb had followed each nameless tendril of water that fed the West Fork into the canyons of the high Cabinets and found its icy source in a little hidden lake or clear cold springs, secret beginnings among the sub-alpine fir and spruce.

Around this face of the mountain, though, and up a steep side canyon was a place a horse would love; a hanging valley that grew mountain grasses thick and green, watered by springs around mossy rocks. The cirque might even harbor a snow bank in the shadows along the south wall, last winter's treasure preserved.

A steep, narrow trail goes up and over the ridge north of the valley, a trail Caleb knew about, but had never taken. Caleb hoped the horse would not find it attractive.

Caleb followed the trail of the young horse to the valley, and there he found him, cropping the grass under the looming cliffs that surrounded the little bottom on three sides.

The horse seemed content to stay in the cirque. He was upwind, and did not hear or smell Caleb and Laban, so Caleb watched for a while, sitting with his glasses trained on the big stallion. He was as fine a horse as Caleb had thought he was, the greatest animal he had ever owned. Even at rest, he was beautiful, as if he had been sculptured. His coat, though dusty and stained from the rigors of the day before, shined honey color. Red highlights in him changed as he moved in the light.

His neck was long and thick, flowing out of a wide, deep chest. He was close to 17 hands, with Morgan lines, a big horse, but there was no denying his grace. In his lineage was Arab or some other dainty breed that set off his heaviness and gave him a touch of majesty. His mane and tail matched the red hues in his coat.

16

In less than five minutes, Caleb knew the check he had given to Hancock was the best-spent $75 he had ever known, but he watched the stallion for the better part of an hour. Then, the wind shifted and took his and Laban's scents across the creek. The gold horse caught their smell and his head came up and swung around into the breeze, looking a little up-canyon from Caleb. When Caleb saw that, he slowly raised one arm and waved.

The horse stared at Caleb and Laban, still about 100 yards away. He snorted, and tossed his head, ran to the back of the meadow and then shied away from the line of brush there, stopped and looked back.

Caleb dismounted and led Laban toward the creek. The horse watched intently, moving nervously up and down the edge of the grass.

"Hey, horsey horse," Caleb called softly. The horse stopped dead still, facing the man with its ears at full attention, and Caleb laughed in spite of himself.

"Hey, old horse," he said in low tones, "want to come home with me?"

The horse did a little dance and kicked up its back legs, and Caleb watched in joy.

AT THE STREAM is a small clearing across from the meadow, a patch of green where Caleb had camped before. Here he stopped and unsaddled and unpacked Laban. He left a rope halter on the big horse and chased him across the creek into the meadow. While the other horse watched, Laban rolled and took a long drink before settling down to eat. Soon, they were both grazing in the afternoon sun, though the stallion was nervous and watchful.

Caleb rolled out his soogan, a canvas tarp folded in half, laced together at the edges and lined with a quilt. When he had set his camp, he went to get dinner. He pulled two cut-throats out of a big pool at the very base of the meadow, just before the creek began its steep stair-step fall down the canyon to the main stream. He moved freely about the place,

17

enjoying its grandeur and the air, and made sure the stallion saw him, heard him, smelled him at every opportunity. From time to time, he strolled into the meadow and approached Laban to pat him, or check a foot, or talk to the big gray. The stallion watched these exchanges intently, but shied away when Caleb came too close, which he would do, ever so casually. When the horse jumped off toward the bushes, Caleb would laugh, and say in his best horse voice, "Hey, horsey horse. You wanta go home with me?"

As day ended, the gray and the gold horse stood side by side in an emerald pasture, moving unconsciously in tandem, casting long shadows that grew together as Caleb sat at his small fire and watched and listened to trout sizzle in the pan.

Night came up the mountain by the same path day had come down that morning. The valley darkened, details slipped into the blue July evening, and the mountain night chill began to creep out of the rock. Caleb ate trout and pan bread with his fingers and cleaned his pans with sand and water and crossed to the meadow for a last talk with the horses.

Caleb was counting on Laban. He knew the big gray wouldn't stray. Laban stood like a rock when a bear walked across the same meadow two summers before. There was plenty to eat. Laban would be there in the morning and so would the stallion, Caleb was betting. Horses are sociable animals. Where one was, another would stay.

In the last light, Caleb scratched the big gray's muzzle and fed him a piece of apple, telling him he was a good old horse. They stood with heads together like two old friends sharing a good talk after a long day. The gold horse looked on and moved in a little, as if to hear better what the other two were talking about. Caleb looked back across the stream to his little fire. The edge of the sky was a band of blue stitched with a few bright diamonds.

Laban pushed his head against Caleb's arm, looking for another bit of apple. Caleb turned to look and found two horse faces looking at him expectantly.

18

Turning slowly, he put a piece of apple in his right palm for Laban, and the gray took it gently. He stretched his left hand out to the stallion, fingers spread, with a slice of the West Fork's best Golden Transparent sitting on his palm. The stallion smelled it, and pulled his lips back and shook his head. Still holding his left hand out, Caleb fed another slice to Laban with his right. After an eternal second, the big gold horse stuck his neck out, leaned forward a little and took the apple slice out of Caleb's hand.

Caleb slowly dropped his arm. Smiling, he walked back across the meadow and crossed the creek to his fire.

SOMETIME IN THE NIGHT, he woke under the canopy of stars. He found Cassiopeia and thought of Sarah. A horse in the meadow nickered softly. Somewhere in the rock behind the meadow, something moved, sending rattling echoes around the cirque.

JASON

ON A CHILLY MORNING, before the peaks around him caught fire, Caleb washed his face at a small clear pool below his camp. The horses had stayed the night. Across the stream they cropped wet grass in the gray-blue light of morning. Behind them, rock rose in black and gray bands to a blue-white sky. The most color of the morning was Caleb's own red cotton shirt.

Hunkered at the creek with hands full of water halfway to his face, Caleb saw the boot print in the moss on the creek bank. Water was still seeping into its depression. He took his time, swallowing back the thrill running up his spine. He knew about how long the track had been there, and whoever left it could be no more than 50 feet away.

He wished mightily that he had his rifle.

Shaking off his hands and running his fingers through his hair, he stood. Calmly, in a conversational tone, he said. "I know you're there. You might as well show yourself," He was sure whoever had left the track could hear him but there was no response.

He sank back on his haunches and stared into the band of bushes bordering the creek.

"Olly, olly outs-in-free." He softly gave the ancient hide-and-seek "all's clear."

There was no response.

"Look," he said, after a moment, "The game is over, and you have been found. I want you to come out now, because you're beginning to make me nervous. I don't like being nervous."

There was no response.

Caleb picked up a small rock and tossed it into the tangle. He gathered larger stones and threw them with growing intensity into the bushes until there came the solid thump and a low yelp.

There was a response.

"All right, all right. Quit. I'll come out." It was a voice not quite matured.

A slender, olive-skinned and dejected young man crawled out of the bushes and stood on the far side of the creek from Caleb, shivering slightly.

He was cold. He had no jacket, and his light cotton work shirt was visibly damp, as were the black trousers he wore. His hair was black and wild on his head, and he had high cheekbones, full lips, and a fine nose between eyes that should have been brown, but were blue, a startling azure in a face that could have been at home on the Eastern Mediterranean.

He looked defiantly and a little fearfully at Caleb. Caleb casually tossed the rock he was holding into the stream and they stood looking at each other without speaking.

Finally Caleb said with certainty, "You're a Wilkins." The boy blinked, surprised. "My mother is. How do you know that?"

Caleb laughed. "Your eyes, son."

He became defiant again. "What if I am? How do you know me?"

Caleb turned and started to his camp. The boy stood watching him go until Caleb waved him on. "Come on, son. It's a long story and it's breakfast time."

However reluctantly, the young man followed at the mention of food, as Caleb knew he would. He knew a hungry boy when he saw one. Whatever this youngster's reason for being here, his plans had gone awry. The cockiness of youth had been thinned by an unprotected night in the Cabinets. At camp, Caleb dug a bulky gray sweater out of his duffel and handed it to the youngster.

"Put it on, son, before you freeze standing there."

"Quit callin' me 'son'."

The young man's voice was muffled and exasperated as he pulled the sweater over his head. Less petulantly, as the sweater began to cut the chill, he said, "Thanks. I was cold."

Caleb poked at the fire and worked the blue enamel coffee pot around to where he could grab it. He poured himself and the younger man each a cup of boiled coffee.

"What's your name, s..." Catching himself, Caleb lowered his voice into the bass scale and said, very officially, "What's your name, mister?" The young man looked carefully at him and found Caleb's blue eyes were sparkling with humor. They both laughed.

"Jason," he said, gratefully sipping at the hot concoction. "Jason Wilkins Indreland." He paused for effect. "And you are a Blascomb."

Caleb was surprised. He looked narrowly at Jason. "You were at the corral yesterday."

"Yes. I saw the whole thing...and figured out who you are."

He looked thoughtful, and sipped his coffee silently. After a minute, he said quietly, "My great uncle used to tell a story about a man named Blascomb and his three sons and a family named Thorton. The boys were Joshua, Aaron, and Caleb. Uncle Jon called them the three wise men. The Thortons had a girl named Sarah, and the Blascombs took the Thortons a miracle for Christmas." He turned his eyes on Caleb. "Is it a true story?"

Caleb looked across the fire at the young man and a little shiver ran across his shoulders. He was ten years old the winter he met Sarah. She was barely six. Smells of oranges and pipe tobacco, liniment and leather came to him, smells from the shop of Jonathan Wilkins in Dillon in the new state of Montana in the winter of 1889. He scanned the ridges around before he answered.

'THIRTY-ODD YEARS AGO, I met Jonathan Wilkins. My second son is named after him. He was a good man. If anyone gave a miracle to the Thortons for Christmas, it was him...and Pa."

The boy looked closely at Caleb, intensely interested. He came around the fire and squatted by Caleb, searching his face. "Are you one of the three wise men?" he asked softly.

Caleb smiled. "I'm Caleb Blascomb." He let that sink in. "I married Sarah Thorton."

Jason blinked in surprise. "You married Sarah?" His voice resounded awe.

Caleb laughed outright. "She grew up, too, Jason."

"Uncle Jon told us the story every Christmas. The three wise men were the bravest boys and Sarah was the prettiest girl in Montana. I always thought ... well, the whole family thought he made it up. But it was such a good story, we made

22

him tell it every year. It's funny, after all this time, to find out it's true." He sounded almost sad.

"I kind of suspected it yesterday, when I heard your name at the corral. 'The horse trader,' Uncle Jon called you. You were youngest, and that made you the keenest trader, because you had to bargain with your brothers."

"El Carim was a prophet, too, I see."

"El Carim?"

"That's what your uncle called himself; 'El Carim.'" Caleb rolled the "r" off the end of his tongue and stretched the "i" into the long sound. "On that Christmas, he traded a winter's supplies for the meager things the Thortons sent to town and Pa threw in a horse and gifts to boot.

"El Carim stepped into a children's game, making miracles for Christmas. He had to have a children's name. It dawned on me 15 years later that El Carim was "miracle" spelled backward and the real miracle of that Christmas was the generosity of my father and Jonathan Wilkins."

"Why do you say he was a prophet?"

"I am a horse trader," Caleb said with a regretful smile, "though Sarah thinks, sometimes, I'm wasting my time and talent."

Jason turned to the horses. He said in a resigned voice. "So, the golden horse is yours,"

Caleb looked at the youngster appraisingly. "Mine if I can catch him. I do have the title. Did you think he might be free to any man who could catch him?"

"I hoped there might be some reward." He let out a small, bitter laugh. "That's not true. I wanted him for mine."

Caleb nodded in understanding. "Can't blame you for that, son." He caught himself. "Sorry."

Jason grinned at Caleb. "I don't mind all that much."

Caleb began to put breakfast together, sending Jason for wood and to the pool for fish. When the first sunlight crept into Caleb's camp, they had cutthroat, coffee, panbread and canned peaches for breakfast, and Jason told Caleb how he came to be on the West Fork.

"I was on my way to Spokane, to a construction job, but I got thrown off the train in Sand River ... at about 25 miles an hour." He ruefully rubbed his rump, and laughed. "But, I landed right, and the bull had enough decency to toss my duffel with me. I found a place to camp, stayed one night, and was planning to catch the evening west-bound before that brouhaha started in the corral.

"He's too much horse not to take notice of, and when the big man went to the chain, I started looking for something to hit him with. That's when you showed up." Jason was somber. "I'm glad you came. All I could find was a piece of pipe. I was afraid I'd kill the..." he trailed off.

"There are a lot of words for men like Dick Hancock, Jason, and one might be 'confused.'" Caleb sighed and shook his head. "I don't think I did much to un-confuse him."

"You did what most of us wanted to."

Caleb chuckled. "I gotta admit, the initial impact felt pretty good."

Jason continued, "Anyway, I didn't hear what you and Hancock had to say after the horse went over the fence, and when you drove off I figured Hancock was still owner. When he didn't start after him, I did. I grabbed a couple of apples and a halter I carry, threw my gear into the brush and into the woods I went. I spent that evening trailing him up here and then all day until you got here trying to get close enough to get that halter on him. Then, you came..." he gave way to silence.

Caleb waited for him to continue, and when he didn't, he asked the question sitting between them. "Why'd you hide, Jason?"

Jason blushed. "Remember when you were a kid and playing and someone would come and you'd get that kind of thrill that said 'run and hide?' It was like that. I didn't want you to know I was here, and the longer I hid, the harder it was to come out, because I knew I was going to look like a fool." He chuckled uncomfortably. "It was kind of stupid, wasn't it?"

Caleb looked sideways at the young man, grinning just a little; trying not to, really. "Only if you mind being cold and hungry and sleeping in the rocks."

Jason grinned back. "OK, it wasn't kind of stupid. It was really stupid." He pointed across the creek. "But, if it would have got me that horse, it would've been worth it!"

They both thought about that for a while.

"He's a canny horse, that one." Jason finally volunteered, looking across the creek to where Laban and the stallion lay warming in the July sun. "I knew he was green, but it took me a while to figure out he was a wild one. He knows the tricks."

"You say he's wild?" Caleb asked, surprised.

"He must have lived wild, at least, maybe was born wild."

Caleb looked at the horse, sizing him up anew, and Jason, too.

"That would explain why Dick was having such a hard time with him, I suppose," he said, nearly to himself, "but he's so well formed, and big. Wild horses, at least the ones I've dealt with, are long on endurance and short on conformity and size."

Jason did not answer this.

"No, Jason," Caleb finally said, "he's not wild. He'd have never stopped here, if he was. He'd have gone on over the top, especially with you after him."

"Oh, he went and looked yesterday morning," Jason said. "He went all the way to the ridge and looked over. I saw him up there and thought I'd lost him, so I sat up there on the big rocks for a while, watching. He went out of sight and came back a couple of times.

"He was deciding something. He stood up there for a long time, and then he came back down to the meadow. He knows how to get out of here. He decided to stay.

"I wonder why," Caleb mused.

"I think I know why," Jason ventured shyly.

"Well, Mr. Horse-mind-reader? Why did that horse come back?" Caleb asked.

Jason laughed, and picked up the pans and headed for the creek. "You're going to think I'm crazy when I tell you."

"That's all right. I kind of think you're crazy, anyway; coming up here with two apples and a rope halter, no food, no coat, after a horse you didn't know from Adam."

Jason was standing with his back to Caleb, a pan in each hand, looking across the stream. Caleb noticed how bow-legged the young man was.

Without turning from the horses, Jason said, "You'd have done it, just like that, if that was what you had to do for that horse. Only difference is that you'll have him."

Caleb frowned. "How do you figure?"

They stood together at the edge of the stream, and watched the stallion clamber to his feet and shake himself in the sun.

"Something started growing in the back of my mind yesterday. He danced around when you spoke to him. I watched him and you all afternoon, and the more I watched, the bigger the thought grew, and when he took the apple out of your palm, it dawned on me." Jason looked at Caleb. "The reason he's still here is because he was waiting for you."

Caleb looked from Jason to the horse, and as if to affirm it, the stallion whinnied into the growing morning.

CAPTURE

I N EXASPERATION, Jason asked, "Why don't you just rope him?"

Sitting in the shade at the edge of a small grove of sub-alpine fir and spruce along the south side of the meadow, they watched the stallion watch them. Two dozen times, the stallion had walked up to Caleb, and an equal number of times, he'd shied from the halter, first the leather one out of the West Fork tack room and then the rope halter Jason had brought up the mountain. The closest Caleb had come was slipping one over his nose, but when it came time to bend the ears under the top strap, the horse shook it off and bolted, running circles around Caleb and Laban while Jason watched.

"He doesn't like halters," Caleb answered, "but that's nothing to how he feels about ropes. Roping that horse would be about like fishing from a canoe and hooking into a whale. You saw him day before yesterday. He'd drag me all over this meadow." Caleb chuckled a little. "You, I think he'd just squash."

"Like hell he would," Jason answered defensively, and reached for the rope at their feet.

"Don't be swearin' at me, son, and don't be making any brash moves toward that horse. Sorry to be a tease. There'll be no more ropes on him. He's just as special as you think he is." He faced Jason and put a finger on his chest. "I have a

27

feeling you're going to be the first one on his back, once we get him to that point ..."

"You're going to let me break him?" Jason was honored.

"I'm going to let you be the first one on him. I didn't say anything about 'breaking'. I just want him to get used to having weight on his back."

"That's the same thing, isn't it?"

"Not quite. I don't break horses. I teach 'em to let me ride. If you beat something into an animal, a lot of times you have to beat them to keep them doing it. My dad showed us how to gentle break a horse, and of all I've worked with, this is the one who needs it most."

Jason was suddenly a little suspicious. "Then, why am I going to be the first one on."

Caleb laughed out loud. "You're getting brighter. You're going to be the first one up because, no matter who it is, or how ready we get him, they're going to get thrown. Your bones will break slower and heal faster than mine ... and I want to watch him move with a rider aboard."

Jason silently watched two ravens soar up the headwall behind the horses, black spots gliding against the multi-colored bands of rock, rising on a sun-fueled thermal to the edge of the sky.

"What if I don't want to?" he asked.

"If you truly don't want to, you won't. I couldn't force you. I wouldn't force you." Caleb said. "Of course, I can't imagine that you might not want to."

Jason laughed, and laid the rope back on the ground.

"When do you have to be in Spokane?" Caleb asked.

"Whenever I can get there will be fine." He paused, looking, it seemed to Caleb, for words. "The boss is my dad. He'll chew on me a little, but it'll be OK."

Caleb looked at him sharply. "You sure?"

Jason nodded. Caleb wasn't convinced. He felt some sort of current there, but he let it go. It could wait a while.

"I want you to ride to Sand River and buy some things, Jason, and then over to the West Fork and pick up an extra horse. You can secure your gear, and be back up here tomorrow by noon. I'm supplied for one, and we're feeding two, and old Scarface over there isn't ready to go home yet."

"Is that what you're going to call him?"

"Don't think so," Caleb answered, "but it will do for now." He considered a little longer. "No, 'Scarface' isn't any kind of permanent name for that horse."

THEY ATE A LUNCH of cold pan-bread, apples and jerky, and Jason went out and caught Laban and brought him back across the creek, leaving the apple cores for the stallion.

Jason saddled Laban. Caleb made a short list of things for him to get from Corbin's Store.

Handing him the list, he said, "Tell Jake Corbin I asked him to let you store your duffel with him. He'll be willing, and Laban and that saddle will be your identity. He knows them both."

Then, he reached into his pocket and pulled out something and put it in Jason's hand. It was a small, oddly shaped, fine-grained red pebble. "When you go to the West Fork, give this to Sarah, and she'll know I sent you."

Jason looked at the little rock, surprised. The stone was roughly heart-shaped, and smooth as much from being in a pocket for years as any reason.

"She found that in the Beaverhead River and gave it to me when she was 11 years old," Caleb said. "There's something to add to your Christmas story."

Jason looked at the rock, and rubbed his fingers across it, then buttoned it into his breast pocket. He swung up into the saddle. Caleb looked up at him.

"Three things, my young friend."

Jason waited, expecting some sort of remonstrance.

"Laban's near to 25. Treat him as a respected old man. Bring back the horse that Sarah picks for you without question ..." he paused, "... and don't lose the rock."

29

JASON STOPPED TO SET THE CINCH and looked back from the spot on the mountain side where Caleb and Laban had first appeared yesterday. Back in the meadow, he could see Caleb and Scarface, Caleb with an arm outstretched and his bedroll blanket over the other. The bridle was under the blanket. The horse stood still as Caleb walked up to him, and he stretched forward and smelled the blanket. Caleb scratched the big horse between the ears.

The scene was one Jason would remember all his life. In that high, green place surrounded by raw rock and sunshine, only a marmot and the birds broke the stillness. The sun was warm, but the breeze out of the cirque was cool.

The stallion, having his neck scratched, put his head against Caleb's chest, leaning against him like a big dog until Caleb lost his balance and fell over. The horse bounded away, dancing in the grass as he had the first time Caleb spoke to him on the mountain. Caleb's laughter pealed like a bell in the distance.

Caleb lay on his back, arms and legs spread like a child on a lawn, exhausted from play. The horse, calm again, walked slowly to the prostrate man, and put his head down near him. Caleb sat up and carefully brought the halter out from under the blanket, and let the horse smell it. He sniffed at it and shook his head, but did not move off. Caleb slowly slipped the leather halter on. This time, the horse did not bolt, and Caleb took his big golden head in both hands, sitting on the ground with his legs out in front of him, broad brimmed hat back on his head, sun shining on his browned face. Even from where Jason was, he could see Caleb grinning from ear to ear.

Jason suddenly felt like a peeping tom. He turned and rode around the mountain side.

SARAH

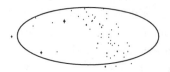

S HE STOOD ON THE PORCH, hands on her hips, angry, it seemed to Jason. He sat up on Laban, self-introduced, but not invited down, and not sure whether he should climb off the horse or not, though he sorely wanted to. It had been a long day and a long ride.

She was not quite what he expected. He had seen her at the corral, of course, but he hadn't known who she was then. He hadn't know that she was Sarah Thorton, heroine of the Beaverhead, rescued in the Christmas tales of Jonathan Wilkins by the brave Blascomb boys from a fate of sure and slow frozen starvation.

He thought she would be prettier, or more petite or delicate; different, in some inexplicable way, than the way she was. At 5 feet and 8 inches, she seemed as tall as Caleb, though Caleb was actually an inch taller, and her slender build seemed more of rawhide than satin. Her dark hair was long and streaked with gray that verged on silver and tied back with a wide pink piece of cotton cloth. She wore a denim riding skirt and a blue blouse, and Jason noticed with surprise that she was barefoot. The single piece of jewelry she wore was a gold wedding ring.

Jason remembered Caleb's finger was also so encircled.

Her complexion was dark and tanned; her hands were large and strong and clean; and her eyes were brown, a dark

31

contrast to Caleb's gray-blue, with crow's feet at the corners, as much there from laughter as too much light and time, Jason thought, but he couldn't be sure. Now, she wore a scowl.

"So, he sent you, did he?" she said, staring in the direction of the mountains. "Where is he?"

Jason pointed to the mouth of the canyon that led to the valley where Caleb and Scarface were. The late evening sun drew out the details of the Cabinets, making the crack in the face of the mountains obvious. She looked a long time. Jason sat uneasily on Laban.

When she turned, she looked at Jason as if for the first time, and then turned back to the mountains.

"You were at the corral the other day," she said. "How did Caleb recruit you?" Her voice, muffled by misdirection, rasped a little on him. Her anger lay close to the surface.

"I volunteered," Jason said testily. It wasn't time to tell the whole story, but he did feel it was time to defend Caleb. "He's up there for good reason, Mrs. Blascomb."

"If you volunteered, I would expect that you think so." Sarah turned her scrutiny to him, skewering him with the tone of her voice.

Jason was angry with her now, "When he brings that horse home..."

"...he'll make the West Fork," Sarah finished for him. She looked back toward the mountains, stiff in the spine and shoulders, her arms wrapped around her ribs below her breasts.

As Jason watched, she seemed to melt a little in the late sun. Her square shoulders softened and after a few moments, she turned back to him, a more pliant expression on her face. She looked sad... and tired. "You must forgive my manners, Mr. Indreland. Step down, come up and sit." She motioned to chairs on the porch.

"William. Jonathan, " she said to the shadows in the front door, "come and put Laban up. See that he's brushed and fed."

The two boys came out into the evening with signs of

dinner around the corners of their mouths. They looked askance at the strange man who came in on their father's horse. A little blonde girl shadowed them as far as her mother's side, and then stopped to spy on the stranger from behind her.

"If you don't mind, Mrs. Blascomb," Jason said, "I'll help the boys. It makes my day feel finished, if you know what I mean."

"That's fine, Mr. Indreland."

"Jason, if you please, Mrs. Blascomb."

For the first time since he had ridden into the yard, Sarah smiled, and Jason knew why she had not been what he expected. The woman with the warm smile who stood now on the front porch was much more the Sarah he knew from the stories.

"A bargain, Mr. Indreland." she offered, "I'll call you Jason if you'll stop calling me 'Mrs. Blascomb.'"

"All right Mrs.…" Jason caught himself and grinned. "All right, ma'am."

"Sarah."

Jason blushed and ducked his head. Sarah sighed and looked away. "All right then, Jason. Put the horse up and come for dinner." She seemed angry again.

He started away, then turned back, digging into his shirt pocket.

"He said to give you this, so you'd know he sent me."

Sarah, frowning, took the red pebble, and turned it over in the palm of her hand with the tip of her finger, as if trying to wake it, a tiny smile at the corner of her mouth.

"Thank you, Jason," she said absently, now holding the stone tightly.

Jason followed the boys toward the horse barn, Bill leading Laban, Jon running ahead to open the side door to the row of stalls. On impulse, Jason looked back.

Sarah stood at the corner of the house, a hand over her eyes, looking off toward the headwaters of the West Fork. The little girl stood beside her, looking from her mother to the mountains and back, trying to see what she saw there. In the last, red light of the sun, Jason thought he saw a tear glitter on Sarah's cheek.

‘**M**OM GETS MELANCHOLY WHEN POP'S GONE,” Bill volunteered, as they put Laban up. Jon monkeyed up into the loft and threw down a fork-full of timothy hay for the horse. Bill brought a coffee-can of oats while Jason brushed Laban and checked and cleared his feet.

"Does your dad go a lot?"

"Nah. Just once in a while."

"Why's your mom get sad about that?"

Bill looked at Jason as if he weren't quite right.

"'Cause. She wants to go, too. Why'd you think?"

"There's no need to be snooty, son."

Bill looked up in surprise, and Jon snorted.

"You sound like the 'old man,'" he said, derisively.

It had struck him too, from a strange angle, that he had sounded like Caleb, but Jason fixed the younger boy with a cold gaze. "Is there something wrong with that?"

Jon looked down, and kicked at the ground with a bare foot. "I didn't mean nothin' bad. It just sounded like something Pop would say."

Jason smiled. "I'd say that was a compliment, Jon. Your pop is a good man."

Jon nodded, mollified.

"Why doesn't your mom go with him?" Jason directed his question to Bill.

"He doesn't ask her."

Bill answered so quickly and so positively that Jason had no choice but to believe that was the reason. The conversation lagged as they finished the barn chores together and then went to the house in the last blue-gray light of day.

‘**W**HY DON'T YOU JUST GO WITH HIM?” Jason asked, mouth full of apple brown-betty. He ate like a man half-starved, which he was after being on the mountain.

34

Sarah considered her answer. To some other, it may have been, "It's none of you're damned business," but for some reason, she wanted to say something to this boy. Perhaps she wanted to hear her own reasons.

She rose from her chair, and walked to the window, squinting through her shadow against the glass into the night. "You'll find, Jason, there are things in this world you don't get to do just because you want to. While Caleb is running off here and there in search of horses, there are children to tend to and things to mend and gardens to keep."

"You sound mad," Jason said.

"I am! You bet I am!" She was surprised at her own vehemence, but the dam was breached. She couldn't hold back the flood.

"While he's up there having an affair with some damned horse, I'm stuck here to 'watch the fort.'" She said it with passion and scorn. "I've been stuck here to 'watch the fort' since God knows when. We used to do lots of things together, but now he seems to think more of his horses than he does of me. He spends more time with them, anyway. And, damn it, I'm lonely!"

She threw it out into the middle of the room for both of them to look at. She was sorry she had exposed herself, but there it lay, a small block of pain. They examined it from their respective sides of the room.

"Do you say anything?" Jason asked.

She was silent for a while. "No. No I don't. It's his business, horses, although I wish he'd do something else. I feel like he's chasing a wild dream of some sort, a dream that will never come true. It's how things are, is all. I just wish things were different."

She felt like crying, and she would later, she knew. But, she also felt better for some reason, as if just saying what she felt was forbidden to say freed her of her thoughts.

Jason did not feel better. He was sorry he had said anything. It was as if he had irritated a festering wound and had no poultice for the pain. It was a familiar feeling.

"You sound like my mother," he said quietly, some deep thing muffling his words.

Sitting now in Caleb's rocker, he drew his legs up in front of him. Rocking and looking over the top of his knees in the lamplight, he looked small and childlike, his blue eyes luminescent in his dark face.

"You do, you know," he continued. "She used to say things like that, and I never knew what to say back. Dad was always working somewhere else, and she was always lonely and complaining. Only, she never complained to him, just me. And, I never told dad 'cause I thought she would."

At the table, he had joked with the boys and teased Alicia. His swarthy face and blue eyes and a story of the road made him seem wise. Now wisdom was replaced by an innocence. Now those eyes were the eyes of a boy, a boy in pain. Sarah's own problems faded into nothingness.

"What happened to your mother, Jason?" she asked softly.

A little smile played across Jason's face, a sad reflection of a smile, really. "We were living in Chicago. Dad was working hard and hadn't been home over seven hours a day for a month. Sometimes, he slept on a cot at work. Mom cried more and more and talked less and less.

"One Sunday, he came home to take us to church. Mom was happy as could be. We all got dressed up and ready to leave and Dad's super showed up at our front door. Dad talked to him for a few minutes, and then he came back to Mom. 'It's my job,' he said, like he was trying to explain, and he went off with the super.

"She packed me and my sisters up, left Dad a note and we went to my grandparents' in New Mexico."

He looked at Sarah. "So, you see, it's not so much of what happened to my mother, as it is a matter of what happened to my dad. We were fine. That was when I was eight years old, and I grew up under my grandfather's roof, loved and protected and raised right. My sisters are still under Grandpa's wing. He's a good old man.

36

"My father never came, though. Not for a long time, until four years ago, I was walking in town, in Santa Fe, and a man standing on the sidewalk said hello to me. It was my dad. I hadn't seen him in seven years, but I knew him. I was afraid, too, that he would take me or something.

"He just talked to me a while, and gave me his address, and told me that he was sorry, and that he would like to stay in touch. He told me he had been a drunk for five years after Mom left, but that I should never tell her that. I never did. She carried around a big lump of hurt for all those years, and that would have sunk her. She loved him."

His eyes were bright. The rocker creaked as it moved. "Dad told me in a letter once that she should have told him. It wasn't an excuse, either. 'She should have told me how unhappy she was, or said something.' he said, 'Then she could have left knowing she had done everything she could.'"

"It sounds like he loves her, too," Sarah said, trying to reassure him.

Suddenly he was the wise man again, blue eyes glittering in his swarthy face. "As much as Caleb loves you, Sarah," he answered.

In the back of Sarah's mind, a bell began to ring. She could not determine what wind moved it, but she did not wait any longer to cry.

S arah had a dream that night. She was standing in a cedar grove, sunlight stepping off the boughs onto the floor of the forest. She was rubbing the big golden horse that Caleb had gone to the mountains for, feeling with her fingers for the scar the rope had left on his neck. She was pleased to find that it was gone, even though the mark from the chain was still on his nose. He wore a new, red leather halter, the one from Jake Corbin's store. A stream gurgled behind her. Standing across the grove in a patch of sunlight, watching her and grinning, was Caleb.

She woke smiling to a dark, damp morning and pulled her riding boots out of the closet.

ESCAPE

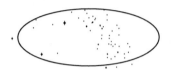

ON THE MOUNTAIN, while Sarah stood at the edge of her porch looking across the miles into the red light of the setting sun, the horse Caleb called Scarface walked to the creek. From camp, Caleb watched him drink and then went out to him. The horse accepted his attentions gladly.

Caleb checked the healing of the gash across the horse's nose and found the infection was beginning to wane. The rope burn around the horse's neck was healing, too. It would be gone before long, Caleb felt, but the scar on the horse's face was another matter. It might be there always.

The halter's nose strap came across the stallion's face a good inch and a half below the wound, but Caleb saw now that it might be a source of irritation. It wouldn't hurt to take it off for the night and allow that much more time free from chafing. Besides, Caleb reasoned, Jason was bringing a new halter of soft red leather lined with sheepskin, one that Jake Corbin kept behind the counter for "just that special horse," as he would say, teasing Caleb for his well-known predisposition.

Caleb slipped the old halter off. The horse, suddenly freed, whinnied and shied away across the meadow. Then, to Caleb's surprise, he started up the trail that Jason had seen him take on his first day on the mountain. He mounted the ridge with such speed and ease and purpose, that Caleb could only watch in wonder. Twenty minutes later, he reached the top. This time he did not vacillate. Over the top he went, leaving Caleb listening to the echo of his single shout of desperation.

"Hey, horse!"

Ten minutes later, it was dark, and Caleb could no longer see the spot where Scarface had disappeared.

As he lay in his blankets later watching the fire die, Caleb had his evening talk with God, and ended the conversation with a long dissertation on the horse before he fell into a fitful sleep.

Later in the night, he had a dream. Sarah and Scarface stood in a lighted grove of cedar along a stream. She was rubbing the horse's neck and talking to him. He wore the red leather halter. Caleb slept in peace for the rest of the night.

CALEB OPENED HIS EYES TO A BLACK MORNING, tinged around the high edges with a hint of gray. It was warmer and quieter and damper than yesterday. It would rain before long.

In the slowly growing day, he found slicker and hat, and lit his coffee fire. Waiting for it to build, he took the tarpaulin that wrapped his soogan and pitched it as a floorless tent on a small grassy hummock back from the creek. Satisfied that it would neither blow away nor flood out, he piled the rest of his bedroll and gear into the makeshift shelter and laced the ends of the inverted "V" shut.

He drank his coffee and ate a cold breakfast, and contemplated the empty meadow across the creek. As he finished his coffee, the rain began. He knew it would be a long day.

IN A CHILL, MISTING RAIN, he slogged to the top of the ridge. It took him an hour to achieve what the horse had done in a third of the time. The clouds were down on the peaks. Behind him in the gloom, little squalls pushed curtains of rain across the mouth of the valley. When he reached the ridge where he last saw Scarface, he was soaked with rain from the waist down and sweat from the waist up.

He stood panting at the top, wispy bits of the bottoms of the clouds whirling by him on the wind. They moved with such swirling speed, watching them made him dizzy. He found only by looking at the ground could he move without tipping over.

He was never to that place before, the divide between the West Fork and another stream to the north. There, the ridge is rounded on top, trimmed off and smoothed down by glaciers which left parallel grooves in the gray rock, using boulders to etch evidence of their passage. Only in cracks does anything grow. Stunted trees cling to the gray, lichen-covered stone like Bonsai trees in a rice paper painting of a Japanese garden.

To the north, as far as Caleb could tell, the ridge fell off into a cirque like the one he just climbed out of, only steeper. He couldn't see far. The rain beat down on his hat, cascading off the brim.

"What in Hell am I doing up here?" he muttered, looking through the rain down the other side. "That horse is gone out of this country by now."

He was not convinced, for some reason. For one thing, where did the horse go? And, how? There was one direction he couldn't have gone. In front of Caleb, 700 feet of thin air separated him from the bottom of the drop.

"A great horse, but Pegasus, he's not," Caleb thought.

He turned west and walked carefully up the ridge. The spine of rock rose and curved toward the north before disappearing into the clouds.

Caleb clambered up the ridge for an hour, watching for signs that the horse might have come that way, until he found himself completely enclosed in the mist. It seemed to flow over the rock like water, pushed by the wind.

It wasn't quite raining, but droplets were so thick in the air, Caleb felt like he was breathing water. He tottered along the ridge talking to himself; trying to keep his balance and his footing against the elements of wind, water and vertigo.

"This is a damn fool thing to be doing, Blascomb."

His voice scarcely reached his own ears for the wind, and a sudden gust tore his hat away. Snatching at it, he fell to his knees on the hard, slick rock, and a sudden, brief opening in the mist showed him how right he was. He was staring into space, the edge of the rock scarcely three feet away. Twenty feet out, his hat sailed lazily on an updraft, spinning slowly and horizontally for an instant before tipping on edge and plummeting out of sight.

Caleb's head swam and his stomach soared. Below, far below, a talus slope ended in a small lake. Clouds floated between the edge of the cliff and the tarn. It occurred to him had his hat stayed on, he would have simply walked off the edge. He was nearly ill.

On hands and knees, he backed away from the edge and sat panting and sweating on the rock, hot and cold by turns, and weak as a kitten. It began to rain, hard. He rolled onto his back and lay there laughing. "Thank you, Lord," he shouted when he had enough strength to shout. He lay there a long time, staring into the clouds, tears and rain rolling down his face.

He sat up after a while, very wet and cold. His legs felt a little like gelatin, but he made a shaky start at walking down the ridge, and as he started down the mountain, his heart sank. He would have to leave the horse for another day, if he was here. He could be laying with Caleb's hat at the bottom, for all he knew, or escaped the other way and half way to the Continental Divide.

The rain diminished to a fine spray as Caleb climbed down to the place he had first topped the ridge. He looked back at camp. Jason had returned. Laban, Sarah's horse Goldie, and Mortimer the mule stood in the meadow. Caleb noted with a smile and a wondrous shake of his head that the wall tent was going up, even as he watched.

"She packed him up for a siege, God bless her. It might well have been, too, if ..."

He looked east, wondering about Scarface. It looked a little more hospitable in that direction. The headwall he stood on descended into a saddle before rising again to a stony peak a mile and a half away. A half-mile east, it intersected another, forested hogback ridge that curved to the north and fell away slightly before disappearing into a lower layer of clouds.

His curiosity got the best of him. Ignoring the cold and wet, he walked down the ridge to the edge of the timber and carefully searched along the edge of the forest. The rain hadn't wiped out the trail under the trees. It excited him to find the tracks there, evenly placed marks of unshod hooves carefully picking their way down the ridge.

Standing there, he visualized what the saddle had looked like from above. He was almost to the intersection with the hogback ridge. He figured....

He stopped the thought from forming. "Tomorrow," he thought to himself.

Today had held enough adventure. He looked again at camp and saw Jason had the tent up, and a fire going. Hot coffee and dry socks suddenly sounded like the world's greatest luxuries. In the west, a sliver of blue was wedged into the gray. He began to work his way back to camp.

42

REPRIEVE

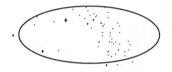

"TOMORROW," SARAH SAID, knowing how badly he felt, "we'll take Laban and Goldie and go after him. He'll be easy to track."

Caleb said between bites, "I appreciate that, but I wonder if by tomorrow he won't be so far gone, we'll never catch him." Then he laughed outright. "Besides, if we start home in the morning, we might save Jason. The boys have him tied to a chair and Alicia is threatening to scalp him with his own knife by now."

Sarah, sitting cross legged beside him at the fire, giggled.

Putting her cup beside her, she pulled her knees up in front of her. "If anyone is tied to chairs, it is the boys and Alicia. They all agreed to mind before I left, which means they won't, but they will stop short of gross insubordination for fear of what will happen ..." she made her voice basso profundo "... when their father gets home."

They ate, sitting in a good silence for a few minutes. Sometimes Caleb felt God sitting right beside him and tonight was such a night, on the upper West Fork with Sarah.

"I'm glad you came, Sarah." He faltered, awkward with his feelings. She had caught him unaware, expecting Jason, not his wife. "I was surprised..."

She snorted. "'Flabbergasted' might be a better word."

"Yes." He laughed about it, imagining his dropped jaw, and he added gently, "But I'm happy you're here tonight."

43

She looked into the fire. She knew she needed to say nothing. She, too, felt God sitting with them by the fire, a part of their party. It was something they had shared since she was an eight-year-old tomboy tracking Caleb on fishing expeditions along the Beaverhead.

It was a special bond they could not explain, nor truly understand. They seldom spoke of it, calling it simply "the Presence" when they did. They merely experienced it at special times, and never, after the first few times they talked about it, had to ask whether the other felt it too.

She thought of the children. It seemed forever since they had been together without the implied threat of interruption. It was 11 years since the birth of William. Before that, there were the years of mourning the loss of their first children; before that, the presence of their first family, the family lost. Now, with miles of distance and seemingly an era of time between them and their tribe, they were at loss for words.

Caleb remembered too. It had been a long time since he had taken cognizant notice of the missing. It was nearly 25 years since the birth of their first child. Mollie had been her name. It was part of their life that was over, but a part that would always be with them, too. Caleb didn't think of it as much as Sarah, he supposed.

Two years before Mollie's birth, on a hot July day in the year 1900, in the front yard of the house where Caleb was born and raised, he stood in a broadcloth suit waiting impatiently in the shade of the big cottonwoods for his bride to appear on the front steps.

Most of the ranch people between Dillon and Virginia City came to see the youngest Blascomb boy tie the knot with Sarah Thorton. There were a lot of disappointed ranch hands and young heirs apparent in the crowd that day, and not a few young ladies who felt they might have been a better choice to wear Amanda Blascomb's wedding dress, but Sarah was the girl who wore it, and at the sight of her, there was not a one who could think it shouldn't be her.

Friends were scarce on the wild Beaverhead. Caleb's

brothers stood with him as "best men." He would not choose between them. Sarah's mother Mollie stood up for her.

The bride's bouquet was of daisies and Indian paint brush and three precious roses from Amanda Blascomb's little garden. Mollie Thorton gave them the hand-braided rug that still graced their bedroom floor. Jack Thorton gave his new son-in-law two heifers and a young bull with big shoulders and lots of promise.

Amanda and Bill Blascomb gave Caleb and Sarah a matched pair of Morgan mares and a young stud colt and the benefit of 11 years of summer-run cowboying, money that Caleb's help had saved them over the years, kept track of and invested well. It was what Bill and Amanda did to send their boys into the world.

They had three children in the following years, Mollie, James, and Jackson, and built a home below the main ranch house on the Abby, nearer the meandering spot where the Beaverhead and the Ruby lose themselves in each other to become the Jefferson. Like the rivers joined, they became one stream of life and days.

For 10 years, the stream flowed without turmoil, without interruption and then, in January, 1911, in the space of two horrible weeks, they lost the children, every one, to influenza.

There was something about that time, the days and weeks that followed. Caleb wondered what had surrounded them, what layer of what grace had protected them both from the entire weight of the circumstance. Thinking back about it, looking back through time, he could see a young couple bereaved, but he could not understand how they could have borne it, all that loss at once.

In all the days and months and years that followed, until they learned to smile and laugh again, and be thankful for the blessing of the day, and in all the nights they held each other against the pain, there was no hint, no thought, no threat of other children.

They left the Beaverhead in 1913, and followed Caleb's desire to live in a place he had seen in travels. They moved over the Divide to the Clark Fork, leaving behind friends and family.

They also left behind a small, neatly-fenced piece of ground on The Arm, the ridge that reaches from the Rubies to the joining of the rivers, where one can stand and see away up the Beaverhead, almost as far as the Thorton ranch, maybe further.

That was the hardest part.

THEY CAME IN LATE MARCH to the Clark Fork, unloading at Cedar Siding, a little place across the river from the land Caleb had bought. It was a cold, gray day. The clouds crouched below the tops of the Cabinets and the Clark Fork was slick and green below the tracks, a different kind of river in a different kind of place. It was too warm to snow, and too cold to rain, but the threat of one or the other hung with the low clouds above them.

Sarah stood apart, looking across the river, arms wrapped around herself while Caleb saw to the unloading of stock and household goods. She paid no attention to the tears running down her face, but Caleb saw. Leading Laban, he walked to her and put an arm around her shoulders.

Stiff and angry, she said to him, "We're cursed, Caleb. I know we are. Why else would God take our babies. Why else would God send us to such a place?"

Caleb was wounded. He had picked the place in summer, with Sarah in mind. He thought she would love it for its difference as well as its beauty. His voice betrayed his pain. "I chose this place, Sarah, not God."

Sarah took no note of his hurt tone. "I hate it!"

He paused and looked across the river, battering back the angry retort that rose. When he spoke, his voice was clipped. "You won't always, Sarah Marie."

She was surprised at his tone, but she remained cold and silent. It began to rain.

Caleb squeezed her shoulder, and said as kindly as he could, "Summer's comin', Sarah. Get your things."

Sarah slumped back toward the train and picked up a suitcase and a cage full of chickens and put them under the canvas cover on the wagon. She turned to go for more, and saw Caleb, shoulders bowed and head down, trudging up the track leading the wagon team. His lips were moving, and she knew instantly he was praying.

In a few more steps, his head came up and his shoulders straightened. She didn't let him see her watching, but there was more spring in her as she went for the rest of the chickens.

And so it went, in that first summer on the West Fork. When Sarah was at wit's end over being lonely and homesick and tired of the work of clearing their new land and tired of having to get by in a tent and tired of never being quite clean and tired of trees and tired of mourning her lost babies, she would cry while Caleb held her, so angry she would beat on his chest, sobbing "We're cursed, we're cursed, I know we are."

And Caleb would tell her that things would be all right, and pray that they would be all right, and after a while, things would be all right again. Until the next time.

TIME AND SWEAT FORMED A HOME in the growing clearing, and Sarah smiled more and cried less. Friends-to-be came out of the forest and up the wagon road, to help, to gossip, to ask a favor. A year went by and then another. Sarah came to love the place she had thought she hated. She and Caleb learned to smile and remembered how to play, as they had along the Beaverhead on those long-before fishing trips.

Sarah had learned to track on the Beaverhead. Tag-alongs have to find those they want to tag along with, even when they sometimes want not to be found.

In her second summer on the Clark Fork, Sarah again took to tracking. It delighted her to follow Caleb. Moving with exaggerated caution, barefoot and fiercely determined, she stalked her quarry. Often she would just watch him work, but sometimes, she would swoop down on him like a hawk on a rabbit. She might simply count coup, touch him and run away, yelling at the top of her lungs like a wild young girl. Or, she might pounce on him and drag him to the ground, wrestling with him until they were both laughing too hard to go on.

Once, she caught him resting on a stump in a sunlit July forest, and came whooping out of the woods, jumped on his back and dragged him to the ground. Straddling his chest, she gave a yell of triumph. Caleb was laughing so hard he could do nothing but surrender.

"Good job, huntress. You've bagged a horse trader."

In mock disdain, she said, "I'll put it back, I guess."

Caleb rolled his eyes. "Can't. You've already taken the heart."

"Yu-uck. You're awful."

"Uh-huh."

Lying on a green mossy spot, both grinning up toward the branches above them, they were quiet for a while. Sarah chuckled and Caleb rolled onto his side and looked at her.

"What?"

"Remember the first day we came here, and I told you we were cursed and I hated it?"

For Caleb, it was an unpleasant memory "Uh-huh."

"Remember what you told me?"

Caleb's quiet, even tone did not hide the hurt well. "That I had picked the place, not God."

Sarah looked at him, realizing for the first time what had hurt him that day. She reached out and touched his face.

Gently, she said, "No, silly, not that. You said," and she lowered her voice, imitating his, "'Summer's comin', Sarah. Get your things,' and then off you walked, as if that was that."

"It was all I could think of to say."

"I know."

They lay silent a while longer. The wooded world of the West Fork buzzed around them.

"Caleb?" she said, quietly.

"Uh-huh?" He sounded almost asleep.

"Summer's here."

Through the branches above them they could see two hawks gamboling in the sky.

TWO AND A HALF YEARS after they came to the West Fork, on a bright October day, Sarah came smiling and told him she was pregnant. There was joy in her eyes. There was peace in her eyes.

They walked across the new orchard, holding hands. "We've been given a reprieve, Caleb."

William was born in May, a fine boy Sarah did not clutch at, nor fear losing, as she might have the year before, and they both knew it was a result of the wait. Time was right for the blessing.

IN A DIFFERENT TIME, on the upper West Fork, Caleb and Sarah sat in warm silence, looking into a small fire, thoughts of days they had lived through entwined, mixed with the smoky incense of smoldering mountain juniper.

Out of this reverie, Caleb sat up straight and started laughing. "Sarah," he said, "did it occur to you when you started this morning that today marks 27 years since we were married?"

Sarah jumped as if shocked, and began to chuckle. Her clear laughter lifted into the night, and mixed with Caleb's and echoed lightly off the rock slides.

They talked then, and as much or more of the present and the future as of the past. They sat up late, and stoked the fire, and shared a cup of rum from the bottle in Caleb's saddle bag, and when the fire had burned down, they went to the tent.

SARAH WOKE IN THE NIGHT. One of the horses called. It was Goldie and she was nervous, by the sound. Then Mortimer sounded off, and Caleb was up, dragging his pants and boots on, pulling his saddle gun from its scabbard and starting out into the night.

"Take your coat, you darn fool," Sarah hissed after him. He came back and got it and kissed her. "Shhh."

She sat in the tent with the blankets wrapped around her, trying to hear over her own heart what might be going on outside. All she could hear were the small gurgling sounds of the creek, the breeze in the trees, Goldie's nervous noises and the occasional thud of a hoof on the meadow floor.

Outside, Caleb strained against the dark, waiting for his eyes to adjust, if they ever would, to starlight. Slowly, the meadow and the things in it came out of the dark a small way into the realm of seeing. It was getting near dawn, Caleb thought. The northeastern rim of the wall behind the meadow showed against a slightly lighter sky. He wished he could see his pocket watch, but didn't dare light a match. When his eyes were all pupil, shapes began to appear in the meadow.

Goldie snorted fearfully, and the shadow that was her pranced around. Something moved on the other side of her that Caleb hoped was Laban, and not a bear or a cat. If it was a black bear or a cougar, Mortimer and Goldie would be gone so far and so fast, it would take a week to find them. If it was a grizzly, it might run one of the animals down. Caleb hoped it was neither. He did not relish the thought of confronting one of the big animals with a .30-.30 in the dark.

Something else snorted, then, some other critter than Goldie, a deep, sonorous sound that was nearly a grunt. A shadow came from the darkest place along the edge of the meadow, moving slowly toward the mare. He cocked the rifle as quietly as he could and prayed for more light. It took Caleb two endless minutes of staring into the darkness to realize what it was.

"WE'VE BEEN GIVEN A REPRIEVE," he whispered to Sarah as he came back into the tent.

"What? What do you mean?"

"Shhh. We don't want to spook him."

"Spook who?"

"Scarface."

"Who?"

"Shhhhh. The stallion. He's back."

"What? Why on earth…"

Caleb chuckled quietly and said in a low voice, "Ask Goldie."

The Talk

THEY WAITED A DAY to take Scarface home. It took Caleb most of the morning to get him to take the new halter, and the fishing was too good to get Sarah out of the creek, though Caleb was sure she was just catching the same fish over and over again.

"Not so," she said, releasing an eight-inch cutthroat back into the stream, "I am merely teaching them to be cautious of what they eat, so big lummoxes like you have to work a little harder for your dinner."

He was sitting on a large rock beside her, lolling in the sunshine, watching her fish.

She took a deep breath. "Caleb," she said, more seriously, "I've been unhappy."

"Yes," he said, quietly, "I knew that."

She looked at him in surprise, forgetting her fishing pole. "Why didn't you say anything?"

"Like what?"

"Well, you could have said, 'Why are you unhappy?'"

"And what would you have said?"

Sarah laughed, a spastic kind of relief-filled guffaw that verged on hysteria, she felt so good.

"God, I am pleased that boy Jason came to visit,"

Jason looked at her through his eyebrows. He started laughing. "You would have said that?"

"I've been lonely, Caleb. We haven't been alone together in years, damn it. I miss you. I miss just being with you. I didn't marry you so we could be separated by business and family. I married you to be with you."

Caleb absorbed this. He felt warm and shy and foolish, like he always did when Sarah declared herself. He felt very, very blessed.

"I want to do more of this."

"Fish?"

"Not just that, I mean all of this." She waved her free arm around expansively. She turned to face him. "Do you know what I mean?"

"I think so," he said. "Yes, I know."

She cast her fly onto the far side of the creek, and let it ride down and around the corner into the pool.

"Well?" she asked.

"Well what?" he asked.

"Well, can I?"

He didn't answer. She pulled a small fish out of the pool, unhooked him and put him back.

"I sound like I'm asking permission." she observed.

"Yes, you do."

She reconsidered her position. "Do you still believe in the horse business?"

Caleb was silent while he considered the question. "Do you think it's time for me to find something else to do?"

"That's not what I asked."

Caleb looked upstream to the meadow where the horses were. "I feel there'll always be a market for well-trained, well-formed, strong, intelligent horses. I've not lost my enthusiasm for it, though I can understand how you may have. We haven't made a killing at it, have we."

"Do you think Scarface is the answer?"

"I've had dreams about that horse, Sarah!" Caleb's voice filled with warm enthusiasm. "He's the most horse I've owned in all my life. If there ever was a single answer to a horseman's dream, he's the one. The colts he sires will ... Sarah, we may never be rich, but that horse will damned sure pay the bills and allow you some of the nicer things you may feel missing."

Sarah smiled at his excitement and allowed herself to believe again in Caleb and the West Fork and the whole idea of their partnership. "When we sell the first colt," she said calmly, "I want to find someone to help at home with the children so you can ask me along on your outings, Caleb. I get tired of being left at home all the time."

"'All the time?'" He didn't feel he was gone that often.

"I want you to ask me to go with you when you come up here, or traipse off to Bozeman to buy a horse, or whatever it is you do when you traipse."

They both laughed.

"Will you go with me when I ask you?"

"When I can," she said, a tease in her voice, flicking her fly across the stream for another run into the pool. She grinned at him and then whooped as her pole bent.

"It's a whale!" she yelled.

Caleb, on his back looking up at the sky, laughed, listening to Sarah battle the "whale."

THEY ATE SARAH'S BIG TROUT and Caleb's panbread with their fingers while Goldie and Scarface played in the meadow. Dignified Laban ignored them, an old gentleman passing lovers in the park. Mortimer, country bumpkin that he was, laughed loudly and rudely in slack-mouthed amazement.

As they cleaned the pans, Sarah asked, "Why do I think I know Jason?"

Caleb chuckled. "He's El Carim's grandnephew."

Sarah was silent as she cross-referenced her mind for "El Carim." Then she was incredulous.

53

"What? How can that be?"

"Jason is Jonathan Wilkin's grandnephew." Caleb asserted smugly. He liked to catch Sarah by surprise.

"How did you find that out?"

He told Sarah about the conversation of the morning before last. "He knows the story. They made Jonathan tell it every Christmas."

Sarah smiled, remembering.

"What's he doing here?"

"Going to join his dad in Spokane," Caleb said, "but first he tried chasing down old Scarface for himself."

"Really?"

"He followed him all the way up here on foot, halter in hand."

"No, the part about his dad."

Caleb looked at Sarah strangely, but she ignored him, looking instead up toward the ridge.

"That's what he told me," Caleb said.

Sarah continued to look across the creek. Mortimer and the horses stood sideways in the sun, absorbing the last heat of the day.

She smiled softly, and finally said, "It will be a good thing."

WEST FORK EDDY

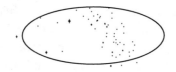

CALEB AND SARAH STOOD AT THE FENCE,
watching Jason work with the big golden horse.
Bill and Jon peered through the lower rails. Alicia
played nearby in the shade of a lilac. The smell of
summer dust and a sweating horse filled the air, and Jason's
soft voice came drifting across the paddock to them as he
reassured the horse.

"There ya go, old horse," he murmured as he lowered a
saddle onto his back. The stallion stood still, not flinching,
not jumping, not moving. Jason reached and pulled the girth
up under the horse's belly, and he merely shifted from one
hind leg to the other. He ran the cinch strap through the rings,
took a deep breath and pulled the girth tight. The horse did
not move. Not a sound came from the group at the fence, but
by Caleb's smile, there might have been a standing ovation.
Scarface was ready for his first rider.

It was six weeks since they'd brought him out of the
mountains. He wouldn't lead from horseback, so Caleb
walked him all the way home. He'd made a lot of progress
since. Now he wore a bridle with a straight bit. He had a soft
mouth and a willing attitude. Caleb loved him all the more.

Jason had gone to Spokane and met his dad and gone to
work. He was back by invitation. Caleb had promised him the
first ride and he was here to take it.

Caleb had done everything he could to prepare the horse for the weight and feel of a man in the saddle, but he didn't know how Scarface was going to take it. Jason was about to find out. He had spent the last couple of days making up to the horse, getting him used to the smell and sound and sight of him, and this morning Caleb felt it was time.

"Here we go," Jason said softly, and put his left foot in the stirrup. He stepped up, tried to swing his leg over, and the horse jumped around to the right in a quick quarter turn. Jason fell back, bounced on his right foot and tried again to put his leg over. Scarface whirled a full 360 degrees to the right, and stopped, being very careful not to step on Jason where he had landed in the dust.

Jason came up instantly, grabbed the reins and faced the horse. Caleb watched carefully for signs of temper in both of them. Jason's face was red, but he wasn't angry as much as embarrassed.

Caleb moved down the fence to where Jason and the horse could hear him.

"Pull his head around to the left, Jason, before you step up. That may hold him."

Jason tightened up on the left rein and brought the horse's head around toward him. He was about halfway into the saddle when the horse exploded to the right, spinning a full half turn before Jason hit the seat of the saddle, bounced and went off the other side.

This time, Jason came up mad. The horse came down facing Jason, ready to jump again.

"Whoa, now, both of you," Caleb said, and climbed over the fence.

Caleb took the horse's head in his hands, held the bridle and faced him full on.

"OK, Jason, try it again."

Jason, looking dubious, put his left foot into the stirrup. Caleb felt the horse tense up.

"Take it easy, old horsey horse," he said, stroking the horse's face with his fingers. "This isn't going to hurt, he's just a feather of a boy, no more weight than the flour sack you hauled around last week. Now, settle down, old horse."

The horse relaxed a little, and Caleb nodded at Jason. "Slow and easy, son. Light in that seat like a dandelion seed."

Jason settled gingerly into the saddle. Scarface stood stock still. Caleb held onto the bridle and talked softly to the horse, giving Jason a chance to get seated and ready.

In a conversational tone, Caleb said, "Hold on, son. He's likely to go every which way."

Jason hooked his hand under the pommel and nodded. Caleb let go of the bridle.

It was hot and still. Caleb saw a bead of sweat pop out on Jason's upper lip. For 10 long seconds, absolutely nothing happened. Then, Jason shifted in the saddle.

The horse went straight up and turned right, spinning and bucking, twisting around on itself almost head to tail. Jason, a good rider, lasted almost five seconds before centrifugal force and the bone jarring jumps of the big stallion put him in the dirt.

Slowly, he climbed to his feet. Scarface stopped dancing and stood warily along the side of the corral, watching and waiting. One rein dragged, and sweat was beginning to show around the saddle. Caleb walked to the horse, calming him with his voice and hands, rubbing him, talking in low warm tones.

"How you doing, son?"

"I've been better," Jason answered, a little angry. He walked stiffly to Caleb and the horse.

"OK, now, be calm about it. A man who's mad doesn't have a snowball's chance in Hell on this horse. Mad is scared, you know."

Jason calmed himself, and talked a little to the horse. "That's why you're jumping. You're scared, aren't ya?"

"You got it," Caleb said, "and he's going to jump again, you can bet." They both laughed when the horse shook his head, nodding in apparent agreement.

"That's better, son. Are you ready again?"

Jason nodded, and Caleb held Scarface as he put his foot in the stirrup. Once again, Jason swung up into the saddle. Once again, Caleb let go of the stallion's head. Once again, the horse stood like a statue.

Gingerly, Jason shifted his weight from one stirrup to the other. The horse stood still. Jason grabbed the pommel and shook the reins. The horse stood still. Very carefully, Jason stood up in the stirrups. The horse stood still. Grinning, he plopped down on the seat.

The ride lasted a full 10 seconds this time, the last seven seconds of which Caleb got to watch from a vantage point on the fence. Jason exited the saddle about two seconds before he hit, temporarily forgetting to let go of the pommel on his way to the ground.

He got up and dusted himself off, bruised but not broken, and limped to the fence.

"He likes to turn to the right," he said ruefully, rubbing a sore spot on his rump.

Sarah, who had joined them at the fence, said, "Just like the West Fork eddy."

Caleb looked at her. "What do you mean?"

"The whirlpool behind the big rock at the mouth of the West Fork always turns clockwise. So does Scarface. He always spins to the right, just like the West Fork eddy."

Caleb looked at the horse standing across the pen, who was looking back across the pen at him, head up and ears up, reins dragging, the picture-perfect image of a ground tied saddle horse, waiting faithfully for his master.

"West Fork eddy, huh? Hey, horsey, horse. Hey, Eddy.

The stallion shook his head and pawed the ground and answered with a whinny.

Eddy never did let Jason stay on very long, but he tolerated Caleb. As a matter of fact, he never dumped Caleb once, though he did try, for form's sake, mostly, and not very hard.

That same afternoon, after Caleb took him around the paddock a couple of times, he and Jason stood at the fence watching him.

"I told you," Jason said "he was waiting for you."

"How come he ran off, then?"

"Maybe you hurt his feelings when you took the halter off."

"Nonsense!"

"He came back, didn't he?"

"He came back for Goldie, not me."

"Maybe, maybe not. I still think he was waiting for you."

They said nothing for a while. The late sun was warm on their backs, but the air was beginning to turn autumnal. Summer would be done soon.

They spoke nearly as one. "I wonder where he went."

They leaned against the rails and searched the shadow-ridden face of the Cabinets for a clue where a horse might go for a night and a day and a night. The lowering sun showed a hundred places and hid a thousand more.

"He turned right at the top of the ridge," Caleb said.

IN LATE SEPTEMBER, Caleb asked Sarah to go for a ride up into the Green Creek valley, a narrow little creek passage with lots of cedar and hemlock and shady places. She accepted and they stopped in a grove of cedar where little patches of sunlight lit the floor under the spreading branches.

Caleb climbed up on a monster tree that had fallen across the valley, seeing if it was solid enough to cross the creek on. It was, and he ran up and down the log like a squirrel, enjoying the height and vantage point it offered.

Sarah ground-tied Goldie and wandered to where Eddy was tied to his training block. He was not quite ground broke, but he would be soon. She rubbed his neck, feeling for the scar of the rope that Dick Hancock had used on him. She was pleased to find it was gone.

Caleb stood on the big log in a patch of sunlight, looking at her, grinning, and they both had a small flash of something in memory they could not quite put a finger on and then it was gone.

"Caleb," she called, "we'll have another child in April."

"Another blessing, Sarah."

"The last one of that kind, I think."

"Yes, I think so too. He must be an important baby."

"'He?'"

"'He,'" Caleb said emphatically, wondering how he knew.

In April, a baby boy was born to Caleb and Sarah. He was a good boy but his brothers and sister tried with some success to spoil him rotten.

The following June, a little honey-colored filly they named Golden Edith, and called Edie, was born to Goldie. West Fork Eddy made the West Fork Ranch a by-word among people looking for a good mountain horse. Edie was the first of them. When she was sold, Caleb and Sarah took a trip by themselves to Yellowstone National Park.

The year before the new boy was old enough to ride alone, Laban, the old dependable gray, was found in the lower pasture, having laid down in the sunshine for the last time. Thomas Jason Blascomb took his first ride alone in his daddy's saddle on a big golden stud horse named West Fork Eddy, and my, weren't they both proud that day. ◆

Intermission: A Short Feature

"The greatest oak was once a little nut that held its ground!"
Quoted from the author's favorite coffee cup.

IF YOU HAVEN'T MET ALEXANDER BLASCOMB, it might help you to know that he is the grandson of Caleb and Sarah Blascomb; the day-dreaming son of Thomas and Grace Blascomb. He was the "ne'er-do-well" of the family and finally the prodigal, a child of God whose ideals and dreams seemed so impossible to achieve that he abandoned them once; betrayed them to follow other people's ideas of what he should be or do or think.

Once, but not for all.

It took him a long time, but Alex finally learned his dreams were God's gifts to him, and his responsibility was to be practical, honorable and tenacious about his duty to God and himself: to build his dreams into reality.

Alex was like many of us, a gamer, though he knew it not. "Never give up" was his motto and his creed, though he often thought of himself as a quitter. He was that man in "It's A Wonderful Life," a 'George Bailey' whose presence was the thing that stood between Bedford Falls and Pottersville, but in his early life, he never had the magic of knowing it.

But someone suspected as much, and sometimes in later years, after she had watched him struggle and triumph and bend in the winds of time to become the giant and battered oak of the Blascomb family tree, she would say to him, "'George Bailey,' I think you've lassoed the moon."

He would answer in his best Jimmy Stewart voice, "Waall, dear, that's nice of you. Now, just what do you think we should do with it?"

And they would laugh and totter off arm in arm to look at a wonder or two. That was when they were old.

PART TWO:

JASON'S PASSAGE

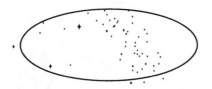

"Something hidden. Go and find it.
Go and look behind the Ranges —
Something lost behind the Ranges.
Lost and waiting for you. Go!"

Rudyard Kipling

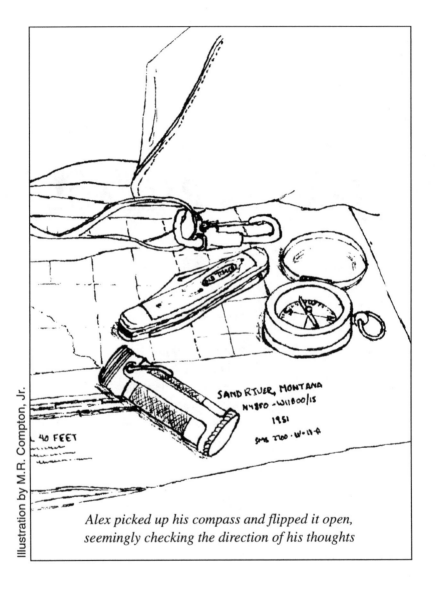

SAND RIVER, MONTANA
N4850 -W11800/15
1951
SMS 2100 · W-17-A

40 FEET

Alex picked up his compass and flipped it open,
seemingly checking the direction of his thoughts

THE HEALING

ALEX WENT LOOKING FOR *THE PROPHET.*
Picking his way through the little store, he felt
wisdom seep like perfumed bath oil into his skin,
cascading from the books along the aisles. The
unhurried search was a supreme act of courage, for the book
he sought was one he had shared with Elizabeth back when
they were in love, a half-million tears ago.

In the depths of the poetry stack, immersed in sunshine
and classical music, he felt at peace, as if he were the bravest
man in the world. Not only did he find Gibran's work, he
picked it up, and read again words they had shared; "...give
your hearts, but not into each other's keeping...." Having read
them, he didn't die of sudden pain, or shatter into a heap on
the floor as he had feared he might.

Instead, he smiled and touched *Gift From the Sea* and
opened a copy. He ran his finger down the spine of a book of
Robert Service's poems, and laughed at the memory of an
argument about the opening stanza of "The Cremation of Sam
McGee." Elizabeth had been right. "The Northern Lights
have seen *queer* sights..."

A volume of Kipling on the shelf reminded him of a
framed needlepoint hanging in a room in a faraway city
where she painted and played her music. He wondered if he
had loved her or her ideas and realized at once they were one

and the same, and the pain was gone and he loved her still.

Nearby was a book of poetry by Lawrence Keith; *Metamorphosis,* which reads upon its last printed page:

> "We must never forsake our Dreams
> For they will find Reality
> The moment we begin living
> In Harmony with Destiny."

H E LEFT THE BOOKSTORE with a sack under his arm and went down two doors to Wilma's World Wide Travel Service. Wilma sold him a round-trip ticket, looking at him as if she had 15 questions about that. He just grinned and winked at her and tucked it inside his jacket. He walked across Three Bridges to the city parking lot, where Walter waited patiently in the pickup, ready for his exciting ride home. Walter, a big, friendly, golden dog, was easily entertained.

Across the lake, Alex could see the Cabinets, white to the top. It was only March after all. The West Fork would be roaring one of these days, as the high country thawed out, but now, only four days into spring, the mountains still harbored winter.

He scratched Walter behind each ear before he climbed into the cab. Sitting behind the wheel, he opened the sack from the book store. He was surprised that he would buy two books for himself on the same day, but his daily morning prayer began "Guide my steps and thoughts today, dear God..."

On that spring day, his thoughts and steps led him to a healing of a small and infinite sort. He started the pickup, and Walter and he began the drive back to the West Fork. Leaping for joy and with a grateful prayer, his heart led him lightly home.

CALLING HOME

AN OLD MARRIED COUPLE sat in their kitchen in Santa Fe, having an argument. He announced over coffee that morning, out of thin air, that he was flying to Montana in the fall to look up the grandson of an old friend. She was not enthused.

Kate was angry at the inconvenience. She'd had enough of his traipsing around the country. She wanted him to stay home and work in the yard and see the grandkids after school. At her age and his, every month, every week, indeed, every day was precious, and to use one foolishly was not a thing she took lightly. Logic was her only defense.

"I don't see why after all this time you need to go."

Jason's gravelly voice was patient as he tried to explain why he was going to Montana. "Caleb Blascomb's been gone 18 years. I've got to do something about this before it's too late."

Kate looked lost, then, and Jason was sorry he said anything about 'being gone.' He often forgot how old they were. He didn't feel that old. Besides, he looked forward to the final step in life. It would be another adventure. But thinking about it bothered Kate.

From time to time, Jason Indreland got an urge and itch that went beyond desire or need or even reason. On a lower pitch than those, like a sub-aural thrumming against his soul, it would persist until he acted. It was such an impulse that led him from Santa Fe to Spokane in 1927, on which trip he met Caleb and Sarah Blascomb.

It was such an urge that led him to court Katherine Black, who spurned him at first. It was 44 years this summer they had been married. All in all, those had been happy years.

Now Jason again felt the itch. He was to go back to a place he had been 64 years before, a high-mountain place, and he was to take Caleb Blascomb's grandson Alexander and someone else with him. He wasn't sure who the second person was, and he wondered if he could do it at his age, but the sound in his soul told him he could and would.

"Kate," he said, "I'm sorry you don't want me to go, and that you don't want to go with me, but I am going in the fall."

She dropped the argument. Katherine Indreland knew that once in a great while, Jason got a burr under his saddle he could neither explain nor ignore, and he would not rest until it was done with. She knew the signs, and this was a classic case. He'd been preoccupied and distant for weeks, and finally had hemmed and hawed his way into an explanation of what was on his mind.

What intrigued her a little was how hare-brained these ideas always seemed, and how she invariably reacted angrily to them, and how they always seemed to turn out all right. It was as if she was a test of his resolve in these matters. If the scheme could not pass the trial of her anger, it was not worth doing. She shook her head.

Jason came to stand behind her where she sat at the table, and put his hands on her shoulders. She patted one of his, and after a bit, he went to the kitchen phone and dialed.

ELIZABETH COULTER slid the ticket out of the envelope for the fourth time since it had arrived at the office, looking again at four hand-written words on the note slipped into the boarding pass slot. It was a round-trip ticket, with an open arrival and departure. "The following restrictions apply," said the fine print. The words in the familiar sprawling script were "Come visit. Love, Alex."

It was the first of his writing she had seen in a long time. She tried to decipher something more out of the words, tried to analyze the handwriting, tried to imagine Alex's motives, and then, laughing at herself, realized that she needn't do that any more. She claimed a small victory over the past in that, and it satisfied her greatly.

She sat at her desk that afternoon a long time after everyone had gone home, working at nothing in particular. She thought and thought and said a prayer, and then went home herself.

'MY, WE'RE COMMUNICATIVE this evening." Margo, Elizabeth's room mate, picked up dinner dishes.

"There's nothing to talk about, really," Elizabeth hedged.

Margo, who could root out a white lie in a room full of raging truths, and whose feelings were hurt when friends tried to hide, sniffed and said nothing. She attacked the dishes with a clatter, and Elizabeth jumped at the noise.

"I got an envelope from Alex today," she said.

"Oh?" Margo rattled the silverware.

"It had an airline ticket in it."

"Oh." Margo quietly wrung out the dish rag. The electric wall clock and the quiet swish of the cloth on the stove-top made enough noise to fill up the quiet in the kitchen.

"That man makes me crazy," Elizabeth finally said.

"I've noticed," said Margo.

"He can't stick to any decision he makes. He's told me good-bye at least 50 times, and then, six months later, here comes another letter. I hate him for his indecision."

"Is that true?"

"Yes. Well, sometimes. I think so." She threw up her hands in despair. "Oh, I don't know."

"Well," Margo said, tongue firmly planted in her cheek, "we know that you never have trouble making up your mind about things."

Elizabeth stuck her tongue out at Margo. "Maybe I'm just

69

as confused about this as he is."

Margo smiled a little sadly, and began drying the silverware. "You know, if he's half the man you once thought he was, you could share that with him. "

Elizabeth did not respond, except to look at her hands.

Margo was repentant. "I'm sorry, Lizzy. I hope that didn't hurt too much. "

Liz shook her head. "'The truth shall set you free.'"

After a while Liz said, "It's not so much him that makes me crazy. It's his persistence. He doesn't ever give up."

"Is that so bad? Persistence is the first step to perseverance." Margo laughed. "Now, there's a scary thought, eh?"

"Not really," Liz said, defensively. Then she giggled. "Yes, it is a little scary. Good God!"

The kitchen clock hummed to itself for about 15 seconds.

"It's his choice of lifestyle. There's no sense of security to it, living out in the middle of nowhere with no real job, trying to ... whatever. I don't even know what he's trying to do."

They went back to listening to the clock.

"Well?" Margo finally asked.

"Well, what?"

"Well, what are you going to do?"

Liz laughed a little hysterically and said through clinched teeth, "I'm going to fly up there and kill him. You can be my alibi. Just tell them that we were together all weekend."

"Someone will surely recognize you from the plane."

"I'll wear a wig and dark glasses."

"Doesn't help Jackie O."

"She's famous."

"You will be, too, if you fly to Montana to kill an ex-husband. The Star will print it up ... 'Mad Woman Exec Kills Ex With Gift Airline Ticket, see page 4. Exclusive photos...'"

"Stop!" Liz was laughing. "You sound like him!"

Margo, who was sometimes as wise as she was perceptive, turned and said, "Did it ever occur to you that you love that man, and that's OK."

Liz stopped laughing.

The first part had occurred to her. The second part, the "that's OK" part, was hard to grasp. Alex's life in his "Valley of the Wild Dream" fell outside of what she considered to be culture's normal pattern. She did not see how she could live there, even if all of the other differences they had could be resolved.

As a matter of fact, resolution of the whole thing was one of the things she wanted most in life, to put their disaster of a marriage behind her and go on. It was hard to do, for she did love Alexander Ezekiel Blascomb, and he was a persistent pest. He was also assuredly not her idea of the ideal man.

"Of course" she thought to herself, "I don't know *what* my idea of the ideal man is. It may *be* Alex.. I wish I knew."

"Elizabeth," Margo said gently, "a visit might help you sort out how you do feel."

Liz jumped. "Mind reader." She smiled at Margo and reached for the phone.

"What are you going to tell him?"

Elizabeth punched in the number. "Off," she said, but she wasn't sure she believed it.

The first time she dialed, it was busy.

IT RANG EIGHT TIMES before he picked up the phone. Elizabeth was about to hang up. Her heart skipped, once, when she heard the reciever lift.

"Hello." He sounded out of breath.

"Hello, Alex. This is Liz."

It was very quiet, and then he said, "I knew that."

She laughed.

"How are you?" he asked.

"I'm fine."

"Calling to make reservations?" He sounded self-assured.

His confidence made her angry. "Calling to cancel, Alex." She regretted it immediately.

"Oh," he said.

She waited for the little boy she knew she'd hurt to speak, but a stranger came on the line.

71

"There's no need to be cruel, Liz." said a gentle, Western voice. It was calm and deep, and a little tired. "It's not your style, and I get my feelings hurt. Are you coming?"

She tried to say no, but something stopped her, a difference in him she did not understand.

"Yes." She said it very carefully, trying to taste the word. It had a funny, sweet flavor.

"Good." He sounded pleased. "Do you know when?"

"Not yet."

"Come in September, if you can. It's a great time of year. If it works out, we can go camping on the West Fork."

Alex hung up thinking what a funny world it was. Two people had called to say they were coming to visit. He'd never met one, though he'd heard the stories, and the other was his ex-wife. It never occurred to him that the two might be connected. He went back to work in the yard, unconsciously whistling, "I'll Be Loving You, Always."

COMING HOME

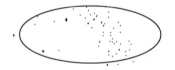

THE 737 SETTLED ONTO THE RUNWAY smoothly. Elizabeth, watching through the window from the plane, and Alexander, watching from the Blue Concourse, wished their hearts, stomachs, and adrenaline levels would drop into a normal position with the same ease and grace.

When they saw each other, they somehow became calm and hugged like cousins who didn't like each other much, shoulder to shoulder, leaning in. They each thought the other hadn't changed much and almost believed it. They found themselves uncomfortable and ill at ease.

Fate came to their aid. A couple in the waiting area picked that moment to begin to bicker about who would carry the camera bag. It escalated to a noisy argument. Alex, mortified, led Liz quickly away from the fray.

"You never did like a fight," she said as the fracas faded behind them.

"You're right," he said crossly, "especially about silly, stupid things that won't matter a damn in 20 minutes."

"Well, there's no need to be mad at me," she said, defensively.

"Liz," he said, not stopping, "I'm not mad at you. I'm just mad."

"Why?"

He slowed perceptibly, and his shoulders sagged. "Because those people reminded me of us, and the world at large, maybe. We're so willing to smack each other for no good reason."

They walked awhile in silence.

"Something else?" she ventured carefully. He had not liked her probing at his feelings.

He smiled. "You're a wise woman, Elizabeth Coulter." He stopped and turned to her. "I'm a little angry at myself because I wanted to say something brave and stunning and altogether wonderful when you got off the plane, and all I could think was that you've changed your hair."

Liz laughed until Alex asked her why. He was pleased at the sound of her laughter and grinned in the shy way she could not help but like.

"Because," she giggled, " I was hoping and praying that you wouldn't say something brave, or stunning, or altogether wonderful, and wondering if you would notice that I've changed my hair."

"Oh," Alex said, "So much for Harlequin Romance."

"So much for the hairdo from heaven," Liz said.

73

Mysteriously and happily at ease, they headed for the luggage carrousel.

Meanwhile, having accomplished much more than they set out to, the couple with the camera case boarded a plane for Denver and made up at 30,000 feet.

THERE IS A TRADITION on the West Fork Ranch started by Sarah Blascomb and carried on by members of the family. If a stranger spends a night under a roof or under the stars on the West Fork, and shares a meal and a story around a wood stove or a camp fire, and comes someday to stay again as many of them did and still do, they are greeted with "Welcome home."

So it was, when the pickup drove between the gate posts that night, that Alex said to Elizabeth, "Welcome home, Liz."

She woke when he said it, rubbing her neck, sleepy eyed, and yawning.

"Are we home yet?" she asked, teasing.

Alex grinned into the starry night, and said only "Yep."

"'Yep?'" thought Liz. "He said, 'Yep?' Who is this guy?"

She stole a glance at him in the dome light as he switched off the truck and opened the door to get out. She used to know. At one time in their lives, Alex had turned from Prince Charming to a frog, right before her very eyes.

Walter came trotting out to meet them and Liz's heart jumped. She felt a sting of unexpected tears. Walter had always been Alex's dog, but there was a short time when he was "theirs," and an exuberant playmate of Liz's. Tonight he seemed distant, accepting her hesitant attention with dignity and deference. She was a little jealous of his joyous reaction to Alex, but neither of them noticed.

In the house, he took her bags upstairs and left them in the extra room. When he came back down, he excused himself.

"I've got to feed Walter and Magic," he explained.

"Who's Magic?"

He grinned at her. "Magic the horse, of course."

74

"You have a horse? Can I see him?"

"Her."

"Her?"

"Her."

"Can I?" She was wide eyed.

"Sure." He was laughing at her.

"What's so funny."

"Your enthusiasm."

"I didn't know you had a horse."

He left it at that, a little perplexed, and they went to feed the horse.

He was, after all, a Blascomb. Horses had been a part of the family for a long time. It occurred to him on the way to the barn that Elizabeth didn't know how deeply that tradition ran in the family, and there were a lot of things she didn't know about him, or him about her. Their short time together hadn't revealed much about either of them to the other. They had too many troubles. In fact, he was not sure he knew this woman at all. He was seeing something he'd never seen before, a child-like enthusiasm, about what he knew not quite, but he liked it. Its honesty pleased him.

In the barn, she laughed at Cat, the barn cat, peering down from the loft, and shyly scratched the horse's nose and poked at Caleb's forge and anvil. Alex, watching, felt she was worth getting to know. In turn, she watched him, and relaxed a little. The monster she remembered, the spoiled boy who had to have his way, was not in evidence. This was a calm and quiet man who seemed at ease with life. They stopped in the yard on the way back to the house and looked at the stars.

A FEW DAYS LATER, there came a knock at the front door, and Elizabeth, reading in the living room, went to answer it. Through the diamond-set square of glass, the back of the visitor's head said only that he was old. Elizabeth opened the door, and the man turned to face her.

"May I help you?" she said.

He was slightly built, perhaps 70, perhaps much older.

Elizabeth could not tell. His eyes looked out of place in his wizened face. They should have been brown. Instead, in the face of a Phoenician were the eyes of a Viking, startlingly blue, all the more vivid for their setting and the age that showed around them, but not in them.

"Mrs. Blascomb?" he asked.

"Uh, no," Elizabeth stammered.

"I'm sorry," the little man said, "but I assumed Alex Blascomb lived here."

"He does. You must be Jason Indreland." Jason nodded. "Please come in. He's expecting you."

"And you are...?"

"I'm Elizabeth Coulter, Mr. Indreland. And, I once was Mrs. Blascomb, but ..." she trailed off.

"... but now, you're not," Jason finished for her. "I'm pleased to meet you."

His manner put her at ease. She laughed that it had been so easy to get over the social hump she had been dreading. "Alex is in back. I'll get him."

"I'll wait," he said, simply.

Liz, after a moment's hesitation, went through the kitchen and out the back door. Jason heard her call Alex's name, her voice fading into the summery afternoon.

In the cabin, it was cool and quiet. The entry room he stood in contained two comfortable chairs with a table between them, a wall lamp and a wood stove of gargantuan proportions. There was an ancient braid rug on the floor, and a six-pane window on each side of the door. It was a dark room, finished in natural wood, a winter haven kind of place. There were coat pegs behind the door, and a boot-drying rack behind the stove.

Doors led left and right from the room. Liz had gone out to the right, through the kitchen. The room on the left was a library. Jason went in, drawn by the books stacked to the ceiling and the light in the place. Someone had been sitting in Caleb's old rocker, reading "The Prophet."

He touched the book and then the wood of the arm of the

chair, feeling its cool smoothness, thinking of his first visit with Sarah on the West Fork, six decades before.

There was a cupboard of keepsakes to the left of the door, lit by a nine-pane window, made of cedar and finished to a gray-red by years of light and use. Photos and knickknacks filled the reaches of recessed shelves. On the center of the three shelves was a black and white photo in a gold frame of a family arrayed against the rails of a corral, all smiling more or less for the camera. A central couple in the photo were the fulcrum of the composition and three youngsters on the left were balanced by a small boy holding the reins of a big horse on the right.

Someone asked, "Do you recognize any of those people."

Jason looked around, surprised. In the doorway was a man about 35, blondish, tan, with his grandfather's blue eyes. He was about six feet tall and somewhere on the slender side of stocky. Jason liked his smile. It was very much like his old friend Caleb's.

"Alexander Blascomb," he said, holding out his hand.

"Yes, sir, that's me. And you are Jason Indreland." He grasped the older man's hand. "I'm pleased to meet you. Welcome home, Mr. Indreland. Welcome back to the valley of the wild dream."

Jason was pleased. "Your grandmother and grandfather live on. It's nice to be here." He pointed to the picture. "Who's holding Eddy here?"

"My dad, Tom Blascomb. That day was his first ride alone."

"Good for him," Jason said. "I spent a total of 28-and-a-half seconds on that horse, though not all at the same time."

Alex laughed. "Grandpa gave you 30 seconds when he told the story. He also told us you weren't much good at hide and seek."

"Olly, olly, outs-in-free," Jason sang, giving the hide-and-seek "all's clear."

"May I come in?" Liz asked from the doorway.

Alex turned and smiled at her. "Of course."

Jason stifled the urge to laugh.

There was a small item in the cupboard Jason noticed when Liz came into the room, but he kept it to himself while he asked Alex about this picture and that, and about the buckles from Eddy's red leather halter. Then he hefted the little souvenir.

"Do you know the story?" he asked

Alex shook his head. "I found it in Grandpa's trunk."

Jason sat in Caleb's rocker and told Alex and Liz a story of Caleb and Sarah Blascomb, the story of the thing in his hand; a small, red, heart-shaped rock picked from the Beaverhead River by a long-ago little girl from Texas.

TRAVEL PLANS

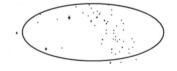

‘T HAT SILLY HORSE STOOD STOCK STILL, until I relaxed and slumped in the saddle and then all Hell broke loose. Around to the right we went, until I let go and landed in the dirt."

It was evening on the lake. Jason's and Elizabeth's return to Montana was celebrated with good food and good wine. Dinner was over. They sat on the deck and Jason recounted the day West Fork Eddy got his name.

Liz was fascinated and amused by the animation of the old man, and a little distracted by Alex, who listened quietly, staring off toward the mountains to the east, an unfamiliar smile on his face. From time to time, his lips moved as if he were silently telling the story.

"At evening, we looked up toward the mountains, watching the shadows form, and we both said at the same time, 'I wonder where he went.' And then we laughed…" Jason paused, his eyes bright with the remembering. Alex nodded, as if in agreement that Jason had told the story right, his smile held in place by joy, it seemed.

They sat in profile, Jason's face superimposed on Alexander's, like two of the mountain ridges that faded away toward the east. Liz had to look away from them for a moment, to keep from crying or laughing, or something. They filled her up with their stories and their presence.

That frightened her a little.

She felt they were looking toward something they could see but she could not. She looked, following their gaze, and there were only the lake and the mountains, things much too large for such a directed gaze. Then she realized they were looking inside to memories, and she felt left out because she had not known those things and at the same time blessed to be sharing them now.

There was also something older than their shared memories between these two men, not quite tangible, but Liz could feel it. They reminded her of father and son, but it went back before Jason, she thought. How far, she couldn't tell, but it was there. A little tingle went up her spine, and she shivered and wrapped her arms around herself.

"Are you cold?" Alex asked.

She shook her head, happy he had asked. She asked Jason, "Where did the horse go?"

Jason answered, "That's why I'm here."

Alex swung around to look at the old man. "To find out where he went?"

"No," Jason said. "I know where he went. I'm here to show you … if these spindly old legs will take me there."

Liz saw Alex look a brief instant at Jason, a strange intensity in his eyes, and then he looked back at the mountains. The smile she was not familiar with danced at the corners of his mouth.

"Old man," he said, and Liz realized it was a title of respect, "you're going to get there fine. If nothing else, we'll tie you into the saddle and let the Magic take you there."

"The magic?" Jason was confused.

"His horse," Liz volunteered. "She's a beaut!"

Alex nearly laughed out loud.

"You have a horse?" Jason's tone was not unlike Liz's of a few nights before, but then he laughed. "Of course you have a horse. After all, you are a Blascomb."

Alex, with that same funny smile, nodded, and said, "Yep, I am a Blascomb."

Elizabeth found herself wondering who this Alex was.

She liked this Alex much better than the last Alex she had known. She felt comfortable with him and was enjoying her stay at the West Fork. It was an unhurried kind of place, and it suited Alex perfectly. He was an unhurried kind of man. She watched him work on fences and firewood, and after adjusting to his funny, swaying walk, realized he moved with grace and purpose, stopping from time to time to...

"To what?" she wondered.

"To gain his bearings," came the answer, "to sniff the air, to find his favorite peak, to marvel at where he is and what he is. To be."

Where that answer came from, she did not know, and did not quite understand, but she liked the answer. Perhaps it was given of God. She had asked, after all.

This visit was not like the ride over fast rapids their courtship and marriage had been. It was more akin to a seat on the bank of a deep, free-flowing river. To step in was to become one with the water on its journey to wherever it was going, and that made her somewhat nervous. She didn't know where the river was going.

Did he? She looked at him. Somehow she thought he did, and in her mind, she put her chair on the bank where she could see the river's course.

He caught her looking and smiled and winked. The expression on her face was "Who is that guy?" He nearly laughed. He wondered himself at times, but knew, whoever he was, he liked him, unlike the guy he had been when they were married.

It was nearly six years since they had divorced, seven since they had married. Why and how they had stayed in touch is a story in itself. Alex told himself at least 500 times "It's over." He told her that. She told him that. They agreed that that was that. They disagreed about whether that was that. But they somehow stayed in each other's minds and hearts. Somehow.

It takes a long time to wear a love like the one they had out. My, how they had loved each other. To the point of self-destruction, to the point of obsession, to the point where it had engulfed them and nearly killed them both.

Elizabeth was strong enough, frightened enough, to end it. Alex fought it tooth and nail. Elizabeth insisted, persisted, resisted...and got her way. God, did she cry over that. And Alex did too. But that was in another universe in time and space, it seemed, on this fine fall evening on the lake. As the day came down to a fine line of pink along the top of the mountains reflected in calm waters, Jason talked about Caleb and Sarah Blascomb and where the horse went.

"The last time I came here before I was married, I found where the horse went. It was in September of the year we caught him. I didn't stop at the West Fork on that trip. I was headed south to Santa Fe, and I worried that I would never get back into the country, so I hiked into the mountains, and went down the ridge, and I found it, by luck ... or Divine Intervention ... or somehow.

"From Santa Fe, I wrote and told Caleb I'd gone back up and over the ridge and found where the horse had gone, and he wrote back and told me to come up sometime and show him. We never got it done. There was always other things." He sighed.

"We kept in touch, your grandfolks and me. I was young and full of myself and couldn't be bothered often, but once in a while, I'd sit down and jot a few lines, and the summer Kate and I were married we came to visit. That was 1947, I guess. We spent a week, and had a wonderful time here. I wanted to go to the mountain, and Caleb and I had it planned, but the day we were going to leave, we had one of the most hellacious thunderstorms I've ever seen. It just went on and on and on, fire popping on the very ridges we wanted to be walking on. Caleb and I sat on the porch and watched and drank coffee and ate most of a fresh dewberry pie to console ourselves, and didn't get to go.

"In March of 1955, out of the blue, I got a letter. Most often, Sarah would write, but this letter was from Caleb. I hadn't heard from them in two or three years, which means I hadn't written in four, and Kate and I had moved to Albuquerque. I don't even know how Caleb found me, but one day, there was a letter from him.

"He said he had a grandson, two years old, Alexander Ezekiel by name. He was his youngest boy's firstborn, a bright little dreamer of a boy, and he wanted me to come and show him the passage someday."

Alex felt as if his grandfather had suddenly placed a hand on his shoulder, but it was Liz who asked, "The passage?"

"The place the horse went."

"Where does it lead?" Liz asked.

"Won't you be surprised," Jason teased.

"Me?"

"You," Jason said. "I can't imagine you'd want to let us go alone."

Alex stood and walked to the edge of the deck, looking into the mountains. "Would you like to go, Liz?"

"Where?"

He pointed. "You can't see it from here. It's over that ridge a couple of ranges."

A verse collected from Kipling long before and kept as one of her favorites came into her mind. Her inner hearing heard it, and she wasn't sure later that her lips hadn't moved with the words.

"Something hidden. Go and find it.
Go and look behind the Ranges —
Something lost behind the Ranges.
Lost and waiting for you. Go!"

Again, that funny, sweet tasting word rolled cautiously off Elizabeth's tongue. "Yes, I'll go."
"Good." Alexander said. "Good. I'm glad."

CONTEMPLATION

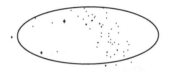

UNDER A CEDAR IN THE FRONT YARD, in a copse between the tree and the fence, was a bench. The seat and back rest were of the same material as the tree, the supporting ends and arms, stone and mortar. It was a shady spot, designed by Alexander's father, Thomas, as a respite against the world that kept him busy. It was a place to sit and think.

Grandparents watched children cavort from this shady spot on summer days. In spring, a tired gardener might rest there after pulling quack grass out of the rock garden that surrounded the cedar and the bed of shade-loving plants.

It was a place for quiet contemplation, where one might sit nearly undetected, a deeper shadow in the shadows under the cedar tree. Jason adopted this spot and in it, watched the comings and goings of the place, thought and read.

The September days were hot. Alex was busy setting aside his early fall work so they could go to the mountains, and Liz was spending a good deal of time walking with Walter. Walter was a large, furry dog, half something big and half something blond. At six weeks old, he adopted Alex as his man. Alex was not thrilled at the time, but Walter turned into a blessing of monumental proportions. He was a calm, intelligent dog of unbounded good humor and unfaltering faith in life in general and Alex in particular.

Liz, Jason noticed, was a little shy of Walter. Perhaps big dogs made her nervous, Jason surmised, but after a day of contemplation he realized the tie between the two was established from "before," and the shyness that Walter did not share with Liz was the result of Liz's reluctance to become attached to the dog. "Reattached" was the word that came to Jason's mind. Walter, 90 pounds of love and joy and boundless energy, was not to be denied. The dog had his way, and the two became a pair.

Liz was enough like Alex to be his sister. She was shaded like him, including her blue eyes. Tall and slim, the whole of her was an extraordinary study in grace. Her smile, which was more of a grin, was contagious as the common cold. When Liz smiled, the world smiled with her.

Moreso, when Alex and Liz smiled together, the Universe smiled with them. In Jason's observation, it happened less than it might have, but more than the two might have suspected. These were friends. But, there was a strain on the friendship.

When Liz, Walter and Alex simultaneously arrived in the front yard, Jason paid extra attention. Walter sensed a tension between the two. He would sit between them, nearly on Liz's feet, and look from one to the other, following conversation like a fan at a tennis match. At the slightest hint of stress, Walter would hie himself off to climb under the front porch. Jason concluded rightly there had been some hellacious fights in the household of Alex and Elizabeth Blascomb.

Once, when a conversation escalated quickly to a point of tension, Alex and Liz stopped to watch Walter slouch dejectedly away, and looked at each other sheepishly.

Alex went down on one knee and looked under the porch. He looked distressed. Elizabeth looked as if she might cry.

"C'mon out, pup. We promise not to kill each other," Alex called softly, "c'mon, buddy. C'mon, Walter."

Walter, reluctantly, clambered out from under the steps and wagged his way across the lawn to the two. He put his head against Alex's chest and Alex ruffed his fur and hugged him.

"We did have some vicious battles, didn't we?" Elizabeth said.

"Yes," Alex said sadly. He looked up at her. "Let's not do that any more."

"People always fight, Alex."

"Then, let's fight fair."

She didn't answer, and Walter moved over under her hand. She scratched his head.

"What would be a fair fight?"

Alex stood up. "One that doesn't hurt."

"Is that possible?"

"We could learn."

It got very still. Jason could hear flies buzzing in the sun and Walter panting. Then the phone rang, and Alex went in.

In the yard, Liz knelt by Walter and Jason heard her say, "I guess we could learn, couldn't we, Walter. Maybe we could learn."

Jason sat in further contemplation.

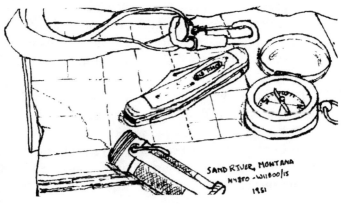

SAND RIVER, MONTANA
NX8F0 -WII800/15
1951

CONVERSATIONS

'W HY DID YOU DIVORCE HER?"
Jason was asking questions.
Liz was in the shower.
Alex was loading his pack.

"I didn't. She divorced me." He stopped shoving socks into a side pocket, a thoughtful look on his face. "That's blaming, isn't it?" He didn't wait for an answer. "We lived through a rough time together, a time when everything that could go wrong, did."

He rolled a pair of jeans and placed them in the main bag. Jason waited.

"There were a lot of wrinkles in our souls, and we tried our best to keep that from each other. Hell, we have probably both spent the last five years admitting those wrinkles to ourselves ... and doing our best to iron them out.

"We loved each other so much, and we were both afraid that if we showed the other one little fault they would disappear in a cloud of smoke." He let out an ironic laugh. "My faults were far from little.

"To top it off, we both had an idealistic, unrealistic idea of what a marriage should be. Being mere humans, we couldn't live up to that ideal and we both felt betrayed by the other and cheated by our own selves. We ended up with no trust or respect between us, just a hopeless kind of love that was both compelling and destructive. Even in that, we wanted to take care of each other, but neither one of us could take care of ourselves. We treated each other very, very badly, especially in the end."

Alex picked up his compass and flipped it open, seemingly checking the direction of his thoughts.

"Neither of us knew how a wife and husband might treat each other. Like lots of people, we ran from one 'true love' to another, looking for God knows what. We were both numb, from too much trouble, too fast. We had it heaped on to overflowing, before and after we met, and only about half was our own doing.

He stopped and thought for a while. "God's saving us for something. That we survived at all is testimony to our tenacity."

"And now you want to do it again?" Jason was puzzled.

"Not on your life. I want a chance to do it right ... with someone. Maybe Liz isn't the girl, but I figure we need to make our peace before we go on. I know I need to.

"So you didn't invite her here to persuade her?"

Again, Alex paused before answering.

"I invited her here to make our peace. In the meantime, I find that I like her ... a lot. She's a friend, by the definition that I trust her and enjoy her company.

"And, I'll admit it. I wanted to see her. I wanted her to see me," he grinned, "in my 'natural surroundings.'"

Jason laughed. "An outing to the wilds for a look at a wild man. What woman could resist?"

"Could resist what?" Liz came in, toweling her hair.

"A wildlife tour of wonderful western Montana," Alex said.

"That sounds like fun," she said. There was that enthusiasm again

Jason and Alex both laughed.

Liz gave them a funny look and went upstairs.

A LEX AND WALTER WENT TO SAND RIVER for mail, extra supplies and dinner. "We will derive maximum amounts of protein and carbohydrates from dinner tonight," he promised.

"That's quite a dog," Jason said to Liz, as the truck left the driveway with Walter leaning on the rail of the pickup box. They sat on the bench under the cedar.

"I wish he'd leash Walter in." It was a "pet peeve," a standing joke, almost, when they were married. Almost, but not quite. They argued extensively about it. Now, as she watched them drive away, she said. "Oh, I don't know why I worry. Walter stays in as long as the tailgate's up. Alex trained him well."

"Why did you divorce him?"

The question came as a surprise, but she knew the answer.

"I was afraid the marriage was going to kill him, or me, or both of us. We had such a rough time of it, and he's so damned stubborn ..." She broke off, sounding angry.

When she resumed, it was with a gentler tone. "Of course, he might have been right, to try to make it work. I don't think we had the skills, though. I know I didn't."

She paused. "He didn't either."

She was quiet for a while, thinking. Jason waited.

"No, the divorce was for the best," she finally said. She turned to Jason. "Do you think he knows that?"

"Yes," he said. He almost felt some tension go out of her.

A few cars went by on the road at the end of the driveway.

"Why did you ask that?" Jason asked.

"I want to know it was the right thing to do. It was so hard. It was the hardest thing I ever did...ever...to watch him try to find his feet and keep myself from trying to help. I just knew I couldn't help without hurting myself...and him. And I was angry, angry at him for not recognizing the sacrifice I was making." She looked down at her clenched fists and realized her nails were digging into her palms. She bit her lower lip to keep the tears back.

"You don't love him?"

"I don't," she said emphatically. Her voice was hard to

find and didn't sound to her like her own. She was feeling defensive.

"Then why are you here?"

"He wanted to prove something to me, so he invited me. That's all." She looked across the yard, blinking hard. "Can we talk about something else?"

They spoke of other things until the pickup rolled into the driveway, Walter's tail wagging above the cab. Alex uncoiled himself from behind the wheel and let the dog out.

He and Walter bounced toward the house.

"But, Walter," Alex said, holding out a potato, "carbohydrates are good for you."

Answering for the dog in a growly voice, he said, "Give me the steaks in the bag, humanoid, or I will ruin forever your lilac bushes."

Liz was laughing hard as Alex disappeared into the house.

Jason headed for the house, saying to himself almost, "What's he trying to prove?"

Liz jumped to Alex's defense, unsure of what Jason would be surly about, but angry. "He's just being Alex."

Jason turned around and winked at her. "Exactly."

S HE STAYED IN THE YARD AWHILE, sitting beside her private river, trailing her toes in the water.

' I 'M FOR BED," Jason said, and went off upstairs to his room, wishing the two at the table good night.

"Fifteen-two, fifteen-four, fifteen-six, and a pair for eight."

Alex pegged his eight, and waited for Liz to count. She had 12 points in her hand and four in the crib, just enough to squeak in for the win. Grinning, she asked "Best three out of five?" She clapped the deck against the table, ready to shuffle.

"I think not, stinker," he said. She had already beat him twice.

"I'm ready for bed myself." He pointed into the air. "Tomorrow, zee mountain vee climb!".

"A French mountaineer?" Liz asked.

"Swiss. Don't you know good Swiss when you hear it? That was my best Swiss, too. Couldn't you hear the holes in the cheese?"

Liz couldn't help laughing. "Alex, you are certifiable."

He smiled, sadly she thought. "Not really, but I've come close a time or two."

It was that same voice she had heard over the phone when she called from home. Home? Was that where she had called from? It seemed eons ago and light years away.

He picked up the board and the cards and put them away. Liz stayed seated.

"You used to get mad when I beat you at cribbage, Alex."

"I did, didn't I. That seems a hundred years ago."

"At least."

There was a pause, punctuated by Walter, scratching behind one ear.

"C'mere, dog," Alex said, dragging out the word to say "dawg."

Walter went to Alex, accepting his attentions with a gently wagging tail.

Finally, Liz asked "Do you remember the letter you sent me, telling me all the things you were sorry for?"

"Yep, I do. Did I miss 'getting mad at you for beating me at cribbage?'"

"No, you remembered everything. That's why I thought of it. It was item number 14, or some such. I laughed so hard when I got that list, it hurt. Which may have explained why I cried, too."

He was quiet, holding Walter's big head between his knees, scratching under his collar.

Finally, he said, "That was a soul cleansing exercise for me, writing that letter, and the others. I hope you understood what I said."

"That you were sorry?"

"That I was sorry, and more. That I was hurt, too." There was that voice again, the one she hadn't known, but was beginning to, but this time it brought a rebelling in her, a rising of the thing that had always said to her, "You were hurt more than he, you gave up more, you sacrificed the marriage for him." It came into the back of her throat, and tried to assert itself in her thoughts.

She looked at him, and he was fooling with Walter's ears, inspecting him. It occurred to her that he was making no accusation, merely stating a way he felt. She got the impression he didn't even expect her to answer. That little smile of his played at the corners of his mouth.

She looked down at the table, at her folded hands, and felt the thing pass away. Peace came over her.

He looked up and she was smiling at her hands, but her smile was trembling.

"What?" he asked.

"I'm sorry, too, Alex," she said. "I'm sorry you hurt."

"Yes, I knew you were," he said, nodding and smiling. "I knew you were. I'm grateful that you can tell me, though. It makes it better." He put his hand over hers and squeezed them, not hard. She noticed that his was brown and strong and wise looking. After he took it away and went to let Walter out, she could feel it there for a long time.

THE WOMAN BY THE RIVER splashed in the shallows, just a little, before she went to sleep.

91

SANCTUARY

THE PICKUP RAISED A RUCKUS and a cloud of dust climbing the rocky logging road to the headwaters of West Fork Creek. The three in the front squeezed left, unconsciously avoiding the abrupt drop on the right. Walter hung his head over the right edge of the box, as if to balance the load.

Jason had decided he could make the trip on foot. They'd left the horse at home.

The road ran around the hillside Caleb had ridden Laban six decades before, and they parked where it stopped, a mile and a half short of the meadow where West Fork Eddy had waited. Walter made sure the world knew he had been there, and then accepted his dog pack saddle with dignity.

The path they took was wide and well marked and passed Caleb's camp spot on the little stream. In the meadow across the creek, they stopped to adjust their packs and have a cracker or two and stayed an hour.

They spent the hour picking up trash.

Jason didn't say much. He and Alex pulled aluminum cans out of the rock fire ring, and put them in a garbage sack Alex carried for such situations. Someone had ignored the "Pack it in, pack it out" sign at the edge of the meadow except to test their hatchet on. Liz picked up plastic bags and six-pack retainers.

The grove of alpine fir along the south side of the meadow where Jason had shivered through a long-ago night showed signs of the ax along its outer edges. The meadow was slowly recovering from a motorcycle race, it appeared.

Jason, finally overcome, muttered a single word into the silence that summed up very well all of their feelings.

It was not a very nice word.

They paused for breath at the top of the ridge, and for the view. With civilization spread out to the south of them, they turned and looked north into the gray and green heart of the Cabinets.

"This is some of the oldest rock on earth we are standing on," Alex said. "When they say 'older than the hills,' these are the hills they are talking about."

"This hasn't changed a lot," Jason said. "Maybe we're all right."

"All right?" Liz was puzzled.

"He's afraid someone has found the passage," Alex said.

"I'm praying they haven't," Jason said. "If they have, and they have done what they did in the meadow back there, they will have desecrated a sanctuary and if they have, God forgive me, I hope they roast in Hell."

They turned right and followed the Forest Service trail down the ridge to where it entered the timber. A few hundred yards later, a hogback ridge went to the left. Leaving the main path, they went through a small patch of bear grass and kinnikinnick and then onto a ridge-top game trail to the north.

It was an easy, beautiful downhill stroll. Great gray pieces of the core of the ridge stuck up through the forest floor, and the trees surviving there on the ridge top did so by wrapping their roots around them, leaving gnarled, red-gray knuckles laying in seams of the rock. The lower country spread out on both sides, showing under the green curtains of the branches of the trees, sunlit and somehow detached by the distance from where they walked, as if they trod a suspension bridge of soil, rock and trees a mile above the earth.

The season was showing. A mountain ash was considering autumn, with just a tinge of red around its serrated leaves. The patches of alder were shot with gold sprinkles, brave fellows leading the rest toward the fall. The place smelled of warm fir and pine needles, but an edge on the air foretold a cold night ahead.

Alex led. Walter scouted ahead. Next came Jason, silent and watchful, looking for clues to a long ago discovery. Liz, who hadn't spent much time in like places, was awed.

For Alex, the lead spot was comfortable. It had not always been so, and he did not fully know why it was now. Maybe it was because he finally had a good idea of where he was going in his life. That had not always been so, either. He had spent many a hike and a lot of years bringing up the rear.

Alex was cognizant of a step over a threshold of faith sometime in the past few years. Others around him took note. Nothing garners faith in someone as much as that someone's faith in themselves. For Alex, it came hand in hand with a trust in the Entity he called God, a funny admixture of religion, intuition, and spirit he could neither define nor deny. He just knew, somehow. As much as anything, this trust was the current Liz could see but not define, sitting on the edge of her private river.

After a mile or so, they came into a place where there was a sort of trough in the top of the ridge. The land rose on both sides of them, more on the left than the right. On the right, they could look under the trees on the top of the trough and see blue sky. Liz wanted to go look, and did while Alex and Jason reconnoitered.

Far below her, down a steep, sometimes precipitous hillside, was a stream. To the south, the direction they had come from, was a small lake that fed the stream, a glowing topaz. Directly east unfolded ridge upon ridge until they faded into blue. North, the stream turned right and cut through the ridges, running east toward some unknown destination.

She sat resting with Walter in the sun until Alex came to find her. He sat beside her.

"Jason says we're very close. He's gone to look for it."

"By himself?"

"It'll be all right."

She said nothing, but she was thinking, and Alex knew it.

"What?" he asked.

"Isn't he a little old to be running around up here by himself?"

Alex chuckled, and put his arm around her shoulders and gave her a squeeze. She thought she might mind him doing that but found she did not. It felt good, as a matter of fact, safe and friendly and reassuring.

"Do you want to tell him?" he asked. They both laughed.

He took his arm away. Liz thought she might mind him doing *that,* but found she did not. He pointed out peaks he recognized, and guessed at the name of the creek below

After a few minutes, Jason called. He still hadn't found it.

"I'm gettin' old," he admitted, a little mournfully.

Alex comforted him. "God didn't get us together to not find it, I don't think, and we've got time. Let's look."

They followed Alex a quarter mile more, and the left side of the trough grew higher until it soared 100 feet above their heads. At a point where the brush between them and the higher ground grew so thick it looked impenetrable, Elizabeth called a halt.

"It's somewhere near here," she said.

Alex looked at her strangely. "How can you know that?"

"I don't know. But whatever it is we are looking for is right here. I know it."

"Wait a minute," Jason said. He saw an argument brewing. "I think she's right, Alex. Just wait here a moment."

He and Walter left them in the vale under the trees and disappeared up-slope into the brush. Alex and Liz followed their crackling movements, and then, suddenly, it was still.

"What did you find?" Alex called.

There was no answer. Liz and Alex had the impression they were alone and Jason had dropped off the edge of the world.

"What the hell ..." Alex muttered, and started into the brush.

"Alex," Liz said. "Wait a moment."

He turned to argue, but something in her face stopped him.

"Just wait. I think it's OK." she said.

He nodded and turned back, listening, leaning into the silence. Liz put a hand on his back, an involuntarily gesture of placation. He turned his head, and she remembered a line from a song, "... there was just a trace of sorrow in your eyes." Then it was gone, replaced by his gentle grin and a wink. Liz found herself blushing.

"Hey. I've found it." Jason's excited voice cracked the moment. "Come on up. Just come right toward my voice."

Liz would have given a million dollars for the expression on Alex's face. It was neither one of surprise nor one that said, "You think your smart, don't you." Instead, he looked at her and nodded and the delight and warmth in his eyes astounded her.

"Good call," he said. "Sorry I doubted."

"It's OK," she nearly whispered.

A steep faint trail led up through the brush, a white-tail deer kind of trail, a lean-over-and-drag-your-knuckles kind of trail. Alex and Liz crawled up through the thicket, nearly on all fours to clear their packs. Alex's caught on the leaning vine maple and serviceberry bushes so much, he finally took his off and dragged it behind him.

Finally reaching a place where they could stand, they found themselves at the base of a small rock slide, perhaps 10 yards wide. At the top, Jason and Walter stood under a mossy rock face, vertically rising to the point they had seen from the vale. On its peak grew a couple dozen gigantic inland Douglas fir, white pine, grand fir and tamarack.

A crack in the rock ran up from where Jason stood toward the top, growing slowly from a few inches to a few feet wide. Jason waved them on and then turned and walked into the face of the cliff, slipping somehow into the seam like a cardboard cutout sliding into a slot in a wall. A canine assistant to a magic act, Walter sat and wagged his tail.

Alex found himself repeating himself. "What the hell?".

They scrambled up the broken rock to where Jason had been standing, arriving in time to hear his deep chuckle echoing lightly off the wall of rock. He stood in the mouth of a miniature canyon, grinning happily.

What appeared from below to be a crack inches wide was a cleft in the rock about four feet across, widening to 12 feet at the top, 75 feet above their heads. The angle of the rock slide, the curve of face of the cliff, and the density of the undergrowth at the base of the slide all combined to make the mouth of the declivity impossible to see unless one was standing practically in it.

Looking into the opening, Liz murmured "Welcome to Jason's Passage."

The bottom of the canyon was rocky, but smoothed by humus fallen from the trees on top of the rock that grew together to form a canopy over the crack. The feet of 100,000 animals had smoothed it out more over 10,000 years. A heavily used trail ran at the base of the cliff. Alex saw there the tracks of deer, elk, goats, coyote, and a large furry dog. Jason saw him taking inventory.

"In 1927, I found the two-month-old tracks of Eddy here. I don't know why they lasted that long, except that rain has a time finding its way to the bottom of this, and he was a heavy animal with small feet. That's why he was such a good dancer, ... small feet." He moved back into the little canyon. "Come on, kids, I'll show you one of the sweetest places I've been. I'll even show you why West Fork Eddy turned left."

They walked back through the crack in the rock, a mossy quiet place that rose slightly and turned slowly to the right. The net effect was that of a long, curving, high-ceilinged hallway. A green half-light in the place gave it a watery appearance, and a slight flow of air gave Liz the feeling that she was swimming against some gentle current. It was about 50 yards before it began to open, the walls subtly moving away from each other to a width of about 20 yards, and then flaring out in a half bell curve on each side.

Encompassed in the champagne glass of which the Passage was the stem the trio found an acre and a half of open timber sitting on a shelf that hung at the edge of a southwest facing cirque. 150 yards wide at its western face, and about 100 yards deep from the rim to the mouth of the Passage, the little hollow was shaped like half a bowl, the edges curving down into a flattened bottom.

Cousins and children of the trees on top of the point grew in open forest. Along the northern edge, birch and aspen grew. Alex found there the reason the horse had turned left; a small spring, a seep of water that was sufficient to attract the animals who had made the trail, and to satisfy thirsty travelers who managed to find a way through Jason's Passage.

They camped there under the trees, back from the meadow that grew at the edge of the cliff. The late sun came in to warm them as they made their camp, and it lit the place clear to the back of the little cirque. Alex and Liz walked to the water together.

Liz was suddenly conscious of the smell of the spring. "I know how I knew, Alex," she ventured.

"How?"

"I smelled the spring. How funny." She was puzzled that she could do that.

"Grandma Sarah could smell out water, too." Alex said. "It's a good talent." He leaned over the pool and set the canvas bucket under a little trickle off the rock.

"It is a sanctuary, isn't it," Liz said, looking at the columns of tree trunks that held up the dark green ceiling of the place. Gold-red light fell among the criss-crossed patterns of the trunks upon each other. The aspen and birch at the spring caught the finest lacing of light on their gold-green leaves, shimmering on a light breeze. Against the gray rock, they looked like inlaid jade and alabaster.

"We'll have to come back here sometime," Alex said.

Neither answered to the assumption.

BACK TO BELIEVING

T
HAT NIGHT AT THE FIRE, conversation skipped
from one spot to another, leading from dogs, where
Walter was discussed, to jobs to children. Jason was
finally led to say, "The generation that grows up in
good times is a spoiled generation. They forget how to work.
They forget how to keep their commitments."

That made Alex mad. "What gives you the right to preach
to us?"

Jason chuckled. "Why do you think I am talking about
you?"

Elizabeth said nothing. What Jason said was true. She had
been guilty of both. Perhaps Alex had a right to be angry, perhaps not. She knew she didn't. She looked across the fire at
him.

"Alex," she heard herself quietly say, "there's something
in what he says. I want us to listen."

He grimaced, but subsided. He looked at Liz, half expecting to see an apologetic look in her eye. There was no such
thing and it pleased him, somehow.

Liz, who was often impatient with Alex's anger, felt her
patience expand. She had more patience here, she thought, or

had her patience grown while she wasn't watching? She wondered if she had changed as much as Alex seemed to have.

She looked at him. He made a funny face. She giggled.

"He hasn't changed *that* much," she thought, but when she looked at him again, there was that unfamiliar smile again, the one she had first noticed at the restaurant.

"Yes, he has," she thought, "and so have I." She brushed her hair back from her face, and caught him watching her, the smile on his face.

There was the river again. She stepped back, but the current remained.

Jason stirred the fire with a stick. In yellow dancing light, his face became a relief map of time. His eyes moved back into the shadows. He did not look up when he began to speak, and when he spoke, it was a litany, a story-chant told by an Old One. Around them, the red fir and tamarack and white pine leaned toward the fire and listened. Behind them, the uncaring shadows danced to shadow tunes played by the wind against the needles.

"It is my job to preach. I have the proxy of your grandfathers," Jason said. "I am their youngest brother. You are my oldest grandchildren.

"I am 83 years old. It is my right to preach. I have earned it. When you are old, you will have earned it, too.

"I've been married to Kate for 44 years. We had our share of troubles. She left me once and I thought of leaving her, but we've been friends and allies most all that time. I engineered the reunion of my parents when I was 19 years old after they had been apart for 11 years. They lived 35 more years together, happy. Not ecstatic, mind you, but happy.

He paused and looked at one and the other. Alex and Liz didn't look up from the fire, but he knew they were listening. He stirred the fire and sparks rose to join the stars as little yellow cousins that twinkled once or twice and were no more.

"Alex's grandparents were together for 73 years..."

"Times were different then," Liz said protesting.

Alex put his hand on hers. "Let's listen, OK?"

100

She nodded silently, looking into the fire.

"Times run from good to bad to good. People learn from the times and from their friends and family. Generations that grow up in good times are often spoiled generations. When something doesn't work just as they think it should, they throw it away and go find another toy. It's been like that for a long time. Times and people, as different as they are, are always the same.

"We came here by a secret way, a passage that is hard to find and easy to miss. Many have walked by this place. Few have been here. Good relationships are like this place.

"A lot of the world walks by the passage that leads to sanctuary every day, but they never see it, never take it. They see it only as a crack that is too narrow to fit through, or leads to nowhere worth going. They take no time to look or explore the possibility. They think it too confining, never expecting the freedom a life apart in such a place offers.

"Both of you know what is right. Friends, family, God, honor and integrity are of the greatest value. You know good work pays good dividends. You know that love, for yourself, your friends and family, even for those against you, is the key to happiness..."

Alex and Liz looked into the fire, listening and nodding.

"...and yet, you haven't believed it."

The indictment was gentle, but it made them look up.

"You loved each other, but you let fear and divisiveness and the words and opinions of others get between you and your God-given dreams. You committed yourselves to the other, but when the going got tough, you gave up. It was easier to get another toy, and not have to try and fix the broken one you had."

Jason paused and smiled sadly.

"Times do change. From what I understand, your divorce was the right thing to do. What is sad to me is that the times haven't taught our children better, so that you and your generation might have avoided the pains you have suffered."

He said nothing for a while, and then he said, "People

change, too, when they make up their mind to. I think you are honorable and tenacious people who have it in them to live the life they want. I think you love each other. I think you might even like each other, God be praised. I think you've each gone off and fixed the toy that is themselves, and that now you belong together again. I think that's what we're all doing on this mountain together.

He poked the fire sharply, sending a small whirlwind of tiny lights into the black sky. "I think that all you need now is to come back to believing."

There was a huge silence in the place that swallowed up the urge to talk, to think, to move. They simply sat. The fire was nearly gone and the shadow dancers had fallen asleep before Jason finally moved silently off to his sleeping bag.

Elizabeth did not move to wipe the streaks that the silent, warm tears left on her face. Only when just a red spark remained did she let go of Alex's hand and move away. She patted Walter good night and went off to her sleeping bag.

Alex, restless, stirred up the fire and moved out to the edge of the place, watching carefully in the starlight for the end of the shelf. When his eyes became accustomed to the dark, he could see the bulk of the mountains crowding in on the valley below. There seemed to be a lightening at the other end, and it took him a few minutes to realize the moon was rising behind him. Walter came and sat at his side.

Below him, a something at the far end of the valley stirred and greeted the moon with a long, low howl.

"Coyote?" he wondered, but thought not. It had been a long time since he'd heard a wolf in the country, but he was sure it was that.

From the near reaches of the valley, in the closer end, another something answered the first. Alexander squatted on his heels on the edge, and marked their movements by the sounds, watching with his ears the two move toward one another. As the moon topped the rock peak behind him, they joined in a joyous yipping howl that led away to silence and sent him smiling toward his sleeping bag.

"Did you hear?" he asked quietly, as he walked past Elizabeth's bed. He didn't know if she was awake.

"It was beautiful," she answered.

Jason, sleepy, but smiling in his bag, said, "Would you two stop the howling and get some sleep?"

THE MOON, FULL AND SILVER, dropped patches of white light on the forest floor in the place, and once, Elizabeth woke to it shining on her face. She got up and walked to the edge and stood in the meadow, looking down at the valley before her. She joined Walter, sitting at the edge of shelf, levering the smell of his cousins out of the night air.

In the stillness of the place, she heard the wind on the ridges around her, blowing through the Douglas fir and tamarack.

She would almost think the next day it had been a dream, but she would never forget quoting Kipling to Walter and the moon or the sound of the wind, blowing across the ranges.

GOING HOME

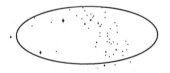

IT WAS RAINING. The thump of the windshield wipers was the only sound Liz could hear above the tires on the highway.

Alex was testy about the rain. "Too damned early," he muttered.

She found herself wishing she had gone on the plane with Jason. They had been back from the mountains for three days, and Alex had not much to say. She didn't know whether to be grateful or indignant, but she was leaning toward indignant. He was reserved to the point of being cool. She had cried putting Jason on the plane. Now she sat against the door, tightly clinching her hands.

They turned south out of Three Bridges, entering the center leg of the journey from the West Fork to Spokane, and Alex began to laugh.

"Damn," he said, "You'd think we were still married."

She looked at him in surprise, but she knew what he meant, and she laughed, too. It had been a familiar scenario between them. At times when conversation was paramount, when there was something important between them to talk about, one or the other or both would withdraw into silence, waiting for the other to make the first move.

"Liz," he began, "I've been a coward these last few days, afraid to tell you how I really feel." He swallowed. "I'm afraid if I tell you how I feel, you'll disappear in a cloud of smoke."

"I promise, Alex, no pyrotechnics. You can search me."

He grinned, and blushed. "Maybe later."

Then she blushed.

"How do you feel, Alex?" she said calmly, though her heart was in her throat. She had no idea, even, of what she wanted him to say. When she felt her nails digging into her palms, she relaxed a little.

When he didn't jump in, she said, "If it will make you feel any better, I'm a little scared myself. You're not the only one who can initiate conversations. We've both been waiting for the other. We have things to talk about. Let's talk."

He relaxed. "It's a help to know, at least, that you haven't made up your mind."

"Alex," she said, a little exasperated, "haven't made up my mind about what? I'm not a mind reader, you know, and you haven't given me any idea about what you want to do, or don't want to do. What have I got to make my mind up about?"

"Hell, Liz, what do you think we're talking about?" His reply was edged with anger.

She started to answer in kind, but stopped and looked out the window.

"Alex, if we're going to fight, let's fight fair."

He smiled, then, the smile that had been missing for the past few days.

"You're right. I'm sorry. I've gotten all tied up in how you might react, when you don't even have anything to react to. Sometimes, I still forget."

He sighed. Liz looked at him in profile. There were light wrinkles on his forehead, and crows feet at the corners of his eyes. A little gray mixed with the dishwater blonde. His ears were too big, sunburned on top. His skin was brown from the Montana summer. His hands were weathered with calluses and scars from good work and bad gloves.

She was seeing him as for the first time. This was not some boy she had loved a million years before, but some man she had just gotten to know.

She remembered a scene from a few days earlier, when they had been back a day from the Cabinets. Alex was showing Jason something he had invented, a moveable fence. From the house, Liz watched the men wave their arms and point and pace, and thought how comical the whole scene was.

Alex was being expansive and entertaining, and she could see Jason laughing at his antics. Alex threw his arms wide into the air, and she heard just the words, said with great enthusiasm "... the whole world ... " and she found herself laughing in spite of herself.

Liz remembered thinking, "Where on earth does that man come up with his ideas?" As hard as some of his times had been, and for all his disappointments, how could so much hope and optimism be tied up in one man? My, how she liked him.

"Alex," she said. "I really like you." She stopped suddenly, echoes of every break-up she had ever gone through running through her mind. "I really like you, but...," was prelude to heartache. Now what would she say? He took her worry away.

"Well," he said, "I'm glad you stopped there. I didn't hear even a hint of a 'but' on the end of that statement."

She laughed, in relief and suddenly liked him more.

"No," she said, "no 'buts.'"

"Elizabeth Coulter," he said, "I like you too. A lot. A whole lot. The final question has been whether I love you or not, and these past few days, I've rummaged around in my heart and soul, moving things here and there, looking under things, and generally muddling about.

"God and I found what I was looking for, under a small shadow of fear, fear of letting go of some old idea of how things should be. What I found is that I don't know if I love you, Elizabeth, and I'm not so sure that it matters all that much. Friendship, I think, is primary. Love? What the hell is it? I've been in love a hundred and fifty times, probably, but friends are hard to come by.

"Maybe real love is friendship extended into commitment. I don't know. I do know that I want us to be friends and live on the West Fork and make love and go dancing once in a while and go on picnics and have a good time. Will you join me Liz? Our lives may take us elsewhere, but that is where I want to start. I want to live that "life apart."

"Who said that?" Liz asked, startled, puzzled, "Who said 'a life apart?'"

Alex chuckled. "Several people over the centuries, but the most recent was Jason, on the mountain."

She remembered; "back to believing."

"Oh, yes."

"Is that your answer?" He was teasing.

"I don't know, Alex," she said seriously. "I don't know what my answer is, yet. I want to think."

"Will you call me when you know?"

"Yes, I'll call you when I know."

"All right, Liz. I guess that's all I can ask."

"Alex?"

106

"Yes."

"I wish I could say more."

"It's OK, Liz. It will be OK."

The truck was warm and the tires hummed and the thump of the windshield wipers seemed to match the rhythm of her heart. Liz drowsed and started and then became the woman by the river, sitting in her chair by the water.

The stream was deep and strong, flowing past calmly on its way somewhere she did not know. She looked down stream to try to see what might lie there, but the river only flowed on out of sight. She stood and walked to the river and for the first time, she looked upstream. Craning her neck, she could see that the river flowed out of the crack in the rock that she had named Jason's Passage.

Somewhere, she could hear Alex singing, "I'll be loving you, always, with a heart that's true, always...."

FINDING HOME

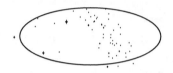

OCTOBER DROPPED OUT OF THE CABINETS on to the West Fork and filled the Valley of the Wild Dream with yellow birches and glazed puddles and fallen orange tamarack needles. The wood shed filled and Magic and Cat put on heavier coats. Walter began sleeping with his nose tucked in. Alex grew restless watching geese fly down the river. The slick-rock country was calling.

"Not this year," he found himself saying, driving the ax into a red fir round. It split so cleanly, so quickly, he was surprised. He pulled another piece onto the block. The knots laughed at him. He thought of Liz, and wondered what she was doing.

"Damn!" he said aloud as the ax fell, and the round flew apart, as if his will split it before the blade reached the wood. He found himself laughing in defense against his aloneness.

Christmas came and went without word from Liz. Alex's mood rose and fell with the mailman, with the ringing of the phone, with each night's prayers and each day's musings.

Huge urges to write or call her came, to pack up his pickup and go south a few thousand miles, and maybe find a job and stay there, if that was what she wanted him to do. The January winds that raged outside the cabin seemed also to rage in his heart and soul.

February came. The storms abated. The winds died down,

and the cold set in, the pervading crystalline freezes that bring a stillness to the world it seems that only death can match. A matching, horrible silence settled into Alex's heart. He found himself at peace, in a resting place, as if the roots of his soul were frozen. At least, he could feel no pain.

March came, and again the winds began to stir. The Chinooks brought a renewed urge to call her, to write, but not the sting of the cold. The silence in Alex's heart melted, the roots of his soul thawed, and a new thought bloomed.

"You know, old dog, sometimes I'm less than smart" Alex said one April day, sitting in the yard, scratching Walter's ears. "I get to decide what's best for me. Why has it never occurred to me that every one else does, too?"

Walter, a wise dog if ever there was one, remained silent.

"...what's best for me..." The thought echoed in Alex's inner hearing and he looked around the yard, smiling. "Going somewhere else just when things are beginning to shape up around here is kind of stupid. I've worked hard for this place. Leaving now for some woman wouldn't be best for me."

Then he laughed a little sadly, feeling a tug at his heart. "And, she is some woman, isn't she?"

Somewhere a long way off, Alex heard a redwing black-bird singing his spring "I'm home from the south" song. The frogs would start their nightly serenades soon, and just after that, Magic could go frolic in the new green fields.

"I wish she were here, old dog. I think she would love today. Hell, she might even like February around here. But she has to decide what's best for her." He headed for the house. "She seems to know that, doesn't she."

In the house, he stopped in front of the picture shelves, studying the people in the gold frame. He noticed the little red rock was missing from its place and wondered briefly which niece or nephew had left it where. He felt sure it would turn up soon and forgot about it.

Unconsciously whistling, he went back to the yard and began cleaning up around the sweetbriar. He felt very good to be home.

AT ALMOST THE SAME MOMENT Alex noticed it missing, Liz, unpacking from a small vacation she had allowed herself, found the little rock in her suitcase, tucked into a seldom-used side pocket. With it was a note in Jason's strong scrawl.

"Dearest granddaughter Liz, I don't know why, but something moved me to plant this in your suitcase. Forgive me if it brings you pain.

"We all must decide what's best for ourselves. Whether you send this back to Alex, or hand it back to him, I think you can trust him and yourself to know that the decision you have reached is the best one for you. There should be no more hearts of stone.

"May God bless you both. All my best, Jason."

She walked into the living room, and Margo looked up.

"Are you all right?"

Elizabeth handed her the note and the rock.

"What on earth?"

"It occurred to me, just now, that I have given no thought, not a tittle or a speck of a tiny consideration to the possibility that I might actually be happy living with that man in Montana, or that I might be happy living without him, too. I haven't thought about it at all."

Liz began crying. Margo stared at her in amazement.

"If I thought about it, I might figure out that I love him and it's OK, and that his crazy "life apart" thing is also OK, maybe even damned attractive. I don't have to go live with him. He's not forcing me. But he is giving me the option ... if he hasn't decided to withdraw the offer."

Liz looked at her friend.

"Margo, what on earth am I going to do?"

"You're going to decide what's best for you, I guess."

"Mind reader."

They talked long into the night about the pros and cons of it all. Liz, exhausted, was asleep when she hit the pillow. Margo lay awake a little longer and asked God to help her friend make a choice.

SOMEWHERE NEAR MORNING, as light just began to grow, Liz had a dream. In it, she was the woman by the river, sitting in a chair back from the water. The stream was deep and strong, flowing past calmly, on its way somewhere she did not know. She looked down stream to try to see what might lie there, but the river only flowed on out of sight.

Then, in front of her, came the sudden gentle broaching of a huge and benign creature through a glaze of calm water.

Liz saw it surface, felt it surface. The size of the beast was not known, nor was it completely captured in the partial siting, but the impression was one of immensity. It slid along before her, exposed by the upper extremity of its passage.

She was not afraid of it. Somehow she knew that should she enter the water, it would keep her safe, keep her afloat when she tired, guard her, protect her, love her beyond all comprehension that she could ever have or hope to have. And, it wasn't a life with Alex the Beast advocated, but a life of happiness for her, Alex or no Alex. Peace and happiness.

She realized she was seeing the back of God.

She stood and walked to the water, and with careful feet, stepped into the river. She was not surprised, somehow, that the water was warm.

LIZ WOKE WITH A START. There was a funny singing in her heart. She remembered the dream very clearly, and she knew how she felt about lots of things.

THE SUN WAS COMING IN THE KITCHEN WINDOW, peeking over the Cabinets. It was May, and Alex was up early, just to see those first golden moments of the day. He was surprised when the phone rang.

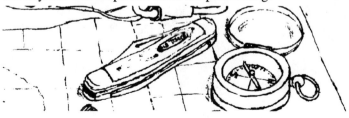

JASON'S PASSAGE

"Work is love made visible."—
Kahil Gibran, "The Prophet."

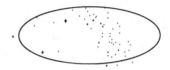

JASON AND KATHERINE INDRELAND came to the wedding, a small and joyous affair, and then they went home to Santa Fe and stayed home. No more traipsing around the world for them. Jason never got another hare-brained idea and Kate thanked goodness for that.

Kate died before Jason, five years after Alex and Liz were married. They went to the funeral. It bothered Liz to see Jason had grown frail-looking, so she stayed on with him a couple of weeks after Alex had gone home to see that he could get on by himself.

"Thank you for looking after me," he told her the evening before she was to fly home. He had a wry expression on his face, and a little smile. He patted her hand across the kitchen table.

"I'm going to be fine, Elizabeth Coulter Blascomb. I've got five more years in me at least. Time to greet your second child." He emphasized "second," and Liz absently rubbed her swollen belly. She felt a flutter. It had just started to do that, something new for her. She graced Jason with her world-moving grin.

"We'll see how the first one goes."

"It will go fine, dear girl."

"It's all your fault. You know that. You and your silly damned rock. I sometimes think you made that story up."

"What if I did?" he asked mischievously.

She looked at him sharply. He was grinning from ear to ear, teasing, she knew. But she wondered, and all the while she wondered, she blessed him for putting the rock in her suitcase.

JASON INDRELAND PASSED AT THE AGE OF 94, five years after Katherine and two years after Elizabeth's second child was born. Of all the things he did, he considered slipping a small red stone into Elizabeth's suitcase and escorting his mother from the train station in Spokane to his father's apartment in 1927 as the two finest works of his life.

ELIZABETH
TELLS A STORY

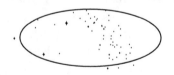

ALL OF THE ADVENTURES AND TRIALS of Alexander and Elizabeth can't be captured here. Those are other stories to tell. Let's just say "Time flies when you're having fun." One day they looked up, and...well, they were tottering around and Elizabeth was telling Alexander *she* thought he'd lassoed the moon.

In those days, they sometimes dreamt of the past, of the adventures and places they saw together in golden reminiscences of simple pleasures well observed. But beside the dreams of the past, there were also dreams of the future. In those days, when Alex and Elizabeth were old, there were grandchildren.

"GRANDMA, TELL ME A STORY."

Elizabeth set aside the brushes and smiled at the blonde two-thirds scale model of herself standing at the entrance of the studio. It was time to take a break. Her back hurt.

It's been a time since you asked me for a story, Lizzie. What brought this on?"

"I want to hear about Alexander and the devil again."

Elizabeth was startled. It was a story Alex told, never she.

"Grandpa's the one who knows that story, Lizzie."

"You know it, too. You know both secrets."

Liz smiled. It was true. She knew the story by heart, and had from the first time she heard it many years before, back when it only had one secret.

It was a parable. There were times when she used it to get through a rough day. The second secret was added spontaneously one creative night by a campfire in their little park on the far side of Jason's Passage. What a special night that had been, back before Lizzie's father was born.

"OK, I'll tell the story…but not here. Let's go in the living room and sit in Grandpa's rocker."

They settled in to the creaking old oak thing, arms worn, upholstery frazzled. They squeezed in side by side, as they had since Lizzie had become too heavy for her grandma's lap. Elizabeth's arms wrapped around her lightly, and like two old friends, they marveled at each other and the comfort between them. They barely fit.

"This is getting pretty tight, isn't it, Grandma?"

Elizabeth had noticed.

"You're growing up, dear." Lizzie was nearly 12.

"Yep. Pretty soon, I'll be able to hold you in my lap."

They both laughed. Elizabeth remembered a long-ago pickup ride with a man who said "Yep."

"Well," she said, "let's see if I can remember the story."

Lizzie laid her head against her Grandma's chest and Liz told her this story:

THERE WAS A MAN NAMED ALEXANDER who was a happy sort. He whistled when he walked and sang in the shower and smiled at his friends and neighbors.

One day, as he went whistling past the Devil's house, the Devil looked out his big picture window and watched him walk by. With an evil little laugh, he said, "There goes a man who is entirely too happy. I'll hurt his loved ones and steal his dreams. I'll wipe that smile off his face for good ... er, for bad."

Chuckling at his own little pun, the Devil set to work.

He found Alexander had a family he loved and who loved him very much. The Devil added a little death and a lot of disease to that picture and helped Alexander trip himself a few times, making relations with the relations strained, at best.

LIZZIE GIGGLED. "'...relations with the relations...,' Grandma?"

"Good joke, huh?"

"Yep."

Elizabeth continued:

A LITTLE LATER, Alexander was looking happy and smiling and telling jokes to his friends, and the Devil said "Darn!" It was his favorite curse.

"GRANDMA," Lizzie drawled, "that's not what Grandpa says."

"What does Grandpa say?" Liz asked, though she knew very well.

"Grandpa says that other word."

"What other word?

"You know."

"You mean Grandpa says 'damn'?" Liz asked in mock horror.

"Yes," Lizzie giggled.

"Well, I'm telling this story, and I'm going to say 'darn'."

Lizzie wiggled closer under Liz's arm. "OK."

Liz continued:

THE DEVIL FOUND ALEXANDER HAD A FRIEND he loved very much, a lady who was to share his life. The Devil schemed and dreamed and sent along a few lies and a lot of fear and scared Alexander's friend away.

"WAS THAT YOU, GRANDMA?"
Elizabeth smiled and sighed. "Yes, I guess it was."

"But you came back."

Liz laughed. "So you know the ending already, do you?"

"Well, you're here."

"Yes, that's true. Now, listen."

And she continued:

A LITTLE LATER, Alexander walked along the path by the Devil's house, smiling and smelling the flowers.

"Darn and double darn," said the Devil. "He's still happy."

Then, the Devil, who knew how hard it was to be poor in the world, took all of Alexander's money and his place to live and his job and worked on grabbing a few other things, like his self-respect and his sanity.

"GRANDPA NEVER SAID ANYTHING about self-respect or sanity, Grandma."

"It slipped his mind, dear. Now hush and let me finish."

Lizzie sighed a huge mock sigh. Liz giggled and continued:

A LITTLE LATER, Alexander came by the Devil's house again, and stopped at the gate and cut a pink rose and stuck it in his lapel and walked away smiling and smelling the rose, whistling "I'll Be Loving You, Always."

The Devil was livid and stomped around the living room yelling and waving his arms. "Darn, darn, darn!" he shouted, "How in the world can I make that man unhappy?"

He sent Loneliness. Alexander made friends and named him Solitude.

'G RANDMA, THIS ISN'T IN THE STORY."
"It is when I tell it, Lizzie. There are certain things your granddad's modesty prevent him from telling. Now, listen, please. This is important."

Lizzie, mystified that something new could be added at this late date, listened very carefully. Elizabeth began again.

THE DEVIL SENT LONELINESS. Alexander made friends and named him Solitude.

The Devil sent Poverty. Alexander transformed him into Simple Means.

He sent Fear. Alexander fought him to a standstill, and he became Courage.

In desperation, the Devil sent Time, the greatest Dream Killer of all.

Alexander turned him into a comrade and named him Patience.

The Devil, who realized the value of his time, quit wasting it and moved on to other victims, but he remembered Alexander.

Alexander and his friend Patience won back the love of his family, and found again that special friend, the one who would share his life. He kept his sense of humor and held his dreams and found success, the kind people recognize only when they have it.

And through it all, he whistled while he walked, and sang in the shower, and smiled at his friends and neighbors.

There came a day when the Devil realized that his fun was over, instead of just beginning.

That day, the Devil saw Alexander standing across a field talking with God.

"So Alexander is dead and headed for Heaven," the Devil thought. Curious as a cat, and knowing Alexander couldn't hurt him now that he was dead, the Devil went to ask Alexander why he never was unhappy.

Alexander listened patiently, with the by-now famous grin on his face, and then pointed at something behind the Devil's back and said, "That's why you always saw me happy, old Devil."

And the Devil, forgetting that Evil must never take its eyes off Good, even for an instant, turned to look over his shoulder.

Snap!

Alexander reached out and broke the Devil's neck.

Now, the Devil hobbles around Hell, a lonely place, looking forever over his shoulder and bumping into walls. He torments himself perpetually for not guessing Alexander's secrets.

The first secret is what the Devil saw over his shoulder. Behind him was God's Veil of Love, where Alexander always went to hide his tears.

LIZ STOPPED THEN, and asked "And what's the second secret?"

Lizzie looked up smiling, hesitant to finish the tale, as children sometimes are, for fear they won't get it exactly right.

From the living room doorway, a deep voice said, "You know, Lizzie. I know you do. Tell us."

Elizabeth Alexandra Blascomb looked over at her grandfather. He had on the smile she loved and the look of calm confidence that made her feel she could do anything.

Grinning, she told the second secret.

"You don't have to be dead to go to Heaven."

The End

Or, is it just *the beginning?*

ABOUT THE AUTHOR ...

MR. COMPTON, JR., known more familiarly as Sandy, was born in Shelton, Washington before being dragged at the age of one to the Cabinet Mountains of Western Montana, "against his will," as he puts it, by his mother and father. Once there, he grew up on a place very much like what he imagines the West Fork Ranch of Caleb and Sarah to be, "only with fewer horses."

JASON'S PASSAGE is Compton's second book of fiction. The novella *CALEB'S MIRACLE,* the first of the Blascomb Family Chronicles, was published in 1991.

COPIES OF THIS BOOK can be ordered by sending $8.30 per copy to CABINET CREST BOOKS, P.O. Box 803, Sandpoint, ID 83864. Postage, tax and handling are included. For information about other writings and future books, send a self-addressed, stamped envelope to the above address.

FOR A COPY OF *METAMORPHOSIS,* by Lawrence Kieth, send $12.00 to 109 Highland, Hope, ID 83836.

THANK YOU, VERY MUCH, for reading *JASON'S PASSAGE.* We sincerely hope you enjoyed it.

CABINET CREST BOOKS